JENNA MOQUIN

SAFE
New and Selected Stories

To my cousin Jessica,
in memory of her
beloved Nick

This is a work of fiction. Names, characters, incidents and dialogue are the products of the author's imagination. Any resemblance to actual persons, living or dead (or undead), or actual events is purely coincidental.

Copyright © 2016 Jenna Moquin

All rights reserved.

ISBN: 1523433914

ISBN-13: 978-1523433919

Cover Design by David O'Neil and Rick Schneider

The following selections, some in different form, were previously published: "Dug Out" in *Asylum Ink;* "Office Politics" in *Heater;* "Newborn" in *Macabre Cadaver* and *The Literary Hatchet;* "The Reward Program" in *Horror Bound;* and "Things That Go Bump in the Morning" was featured on *Inkitt*

CONTENTS

The End of a Marriage 9
Newborn 20
The Machine 32
Office Politics 38
The Heaven or Hell Line 46
Dug Out 59
Casualtites of Encounters 73
The Donation 97
Safe 135
Waiting Room 144
The Reward Program 166
Things That Go Bump in the Morning 173
Indictment 183
The Dark Gland 192
The Sublime Life 203

The End of a Marriage

Carter Lloyd sat in the garage underneath the high-rise where he lived with his wife Georgia. He knew she was upstairs fixing dinner, and he sat in his car wondering exactly how he was going to say that he was leaving her for another woman.

A few months ago his company assigned him to recruit at a job fair at Northeastern University. Sarah walked up to his booth with her long, shiny black hair and eyes that were almost violet, like Elizabeth Taylor's.

He told Sarah he was separated, though back then he had no intention of leaving his wife. It wasn't until he spent time with Sarah that the idea of marrying a younger woman began to appeal to him. Her biological clock wouldn't tick for a few years, and lately Georgia would only have sex with him when she was ovulating.

Carter sighed and glanced at his watch, a birthday gift from his wealthy mother-in-law. If he hadn't already made a fortune in pharmaceuticals, he would stay with Georgia for her family money. But he felt more independent and free lately, and Sarah had a lot to do with that. She reminded him of how Georgia was when they first met. Fun, sexy, full of laughter and filled him with hope for the future.

Over the years, Georgia changed into someone he didn't recognize. He thought about how she followed him around with a sponge whenever he ate a cookie. The way she ironed everything, including his boxer shorts. How she scolded him every time he cursed.

He couldn't understand how the sassy, free-spirited girl he'd fallen for in college had morphed into someone so conservative and delicate. Part of him had an overwhelming sense of resentment toward her for turning into someone different. He wanted her to stay the same, and he'd found in Sarah what Georgia used to be.

Carter stepped out of the car and locked it with a beep from the key fob. He walked to the elevator and rode it to the fifteenth floor.

He pictured the different reactions from Georgia as he stood in the elevator. Crying, or possibly hyperventilating. Though she wasn't the type to get violent, she could easily get hysterical over something like this. He hoped she would just want a divorce, but he doubted that reaction.

If she wouldn't agree to a divorce, and got too hysterical to the point of threatening her life or his, Carter had a backup plan. He fingered the revolver inside the pocket of his jacket.

As he approached the door, he heard Georgia humming. He thought she had an annoyingly loud hum, and it was something she always did while doing household chores. It sounded like she was humming the tune of "Oh! Susanna" but it was hard to hear clearly through the door. He took a deep breath and walked inside.

"Carter?" Georgia called from the kitchen.

"Hi, sweetie!"

He was worried his voice sounded overly cheerful. Sweat poured down the back of his neck. He slipped out of his jacket when he reached the coat rack and felt the weight of the gun. He patted it as he hung the jacket and told himself it was a last resort.

The End of a Marriage

Carter clenched and unclenched his hands during the walk to the kitchen. He passed Georgia's potted plants, and a picture of them on the log ride at some amusement park years ago. He couldn't recall which park.

He took several deep breaths as he watched his wife chop carrots on the cutting board. He looked at Georgia's ginger hair that was curled at the bottom and held back by a blindingly white headband. Her lavender blouse was buttoned almost to the top, the lace on the collar matching the lace that trimmed her apron. The pearls that his mother gave her on their wedding day, that Georgia took pride in wearing as often as possible. To Carter, she looked like the type of woman labeled "The Perfect Housewife" in some 1950s edition of *House & Garden.*

"Dinner will be ready soon. I'm just working on the salad." Georgia smiled at him.

"Sounds good." Carter grabbed a napkin and wiped the back of his neck.

"Are you feeling hot? Want me to turn on the air conditioning?"

"No, I'm ok. I was actually hoping we could talk."

Georgia looked at him with her eyebrows raised and gave him a faint smile. She tossed the carrots into the salad bowl and picked up a large cucumber.

"What would you like to talk about, sweetie?"

She grasped the cucumber in one hand, peeler in the other, and in a manner of seconds had peeled it completely. She placed the cucumber on the cutting board and picked up the knife. She chopped with her eyes on Carter.

He eyed the way she chopped and diced and realized he never noticed before how deftly she used the knife.

"Could you stop for a minute, please?"

"Is something wrong?" She tossed the cucumber pieces into the salad.

"I, well I, Georgia…there's something I need to talk to you about."

"Yes, you said that already. And now I'm worried. What's the matter?"

Carter sighed and pulled out one of the stools stored underneath the kitchen island. He sat down and placed his chin into his cupped hands and closed his eyes.

"I'm not sure how to tell you this. I guess I'll just come out and say it."

Georgia narrowed her eyes. Though she had ceased preparing the salad, she still held onto the knife.

"I fell in love with another woman."

Georgia's grip on the knife tightened, and she sucked in a deep breath. Carter opened his eyes, and saw a reaction he hadn't even considered.

The corners of her mouth turned up slightly in a smile. Then she set down the knife, chuckled and tossed the salad with large wooden tongs.

"When we first met, I knew you were a womanizer. Everyone warned me, they said 'Carter will never settle down with one woman,' and I laughed it off. I was just a girl then."

"Georgia, you were the woman I wanted as my wife…you were the perfect wife! Almost a bit too perfect."

He started to relax. He picked up a piece of cucumber that had remained on the cutting board and tossed it into his mouth.

"I started to suspect things about a year after our honeymoon," Georgia continued. "But I didn't start following you until I saw the text message from Clementine."

Carter froze and his already pale skin whitened. Clementine was a girl he'd met a few years ago. She worked at Victoria's Secret and flirted with him when he came in to buy a camisole for Georgia, who never did wear it. They had an affair that lasted six months, and then Clementine stopped returning his calls and messages. He went to the mall looking for her, and her manager told him she'd quit and moved back home to Phoenix.

"Clementine? I don't know what you're talking about…"

"Don't lie to me!"

Georgia shrieked so loudly Carter flinched. She picked the knife back up and threw it at him. He ducked and the blade stuck into the wall.

"There was Clementine, and then Susanna…you seemed to have a thing for women named after old country songs. This latest one at least has a classy name, Sarah Morella. Is that Italian?"

"You…you knew about Susanna? And Sarah?"

Carter inched away from the knife in the wall and his stomach churned. He wondered if she poisoned the cucumber. Georgia smirked as she took another knife from the drawer.

"Do you remember what happened with Clementine and Susanna?"

"They both got sick of me and took off," he said and threw his hands up in the air.

"Well, that's not exactly what happened." Georgia laughed.

"What's so funny?"

"You see Carter, I had something to do with their…disappearances."

Carter's eyes widened as he gripped the edge of the counter.

"What did you do?"

"After I saw your text to Clementine about meeting at the café, I kept you from going there and went to meet her myself."

"What do you mean?"

"Do you remember when I asked you to pick up my mother at the doctor's, but when you got there my brother had already picked her up?"

Carter nodded.

"I sent you on that fake errand to buy some time so I could go and meet Clementine that night. I went to the café, and saw her sitting at a table waiting for you, looking just as trampy as the photos I found in your phone. I sat across from her and introduced myself. She tried to get up but I grabbed her hand, and in my other hand I had a small knife. Luckily for me that café where you always met your mistresses was so dim inside, no one could tell what was going on."

"What did you do?"

"I pressed the knife against her chin and told her that she was to leave town that night, and never come back. And if I caught her with you again, I would stab a knife into every part of her body where I could see a vein through that fair skin."

Carter's breathing quickened. His wife knowing about his affairs was hard enough to stomach. But learning that she'd meddled in them like this was making his pulse race so hard it felt like his blood was boiling. His face grew hot and he desperately wanted a drink. He swallowed down a lump in his throat, burped and tasted cucumber.

The End of a Marriage

"What about Susanna?" He asked although he wasn't quite sure he wanted to know the answer.

"Oh! Susanna," she said with a laugh. "She was a tough one. I knew she wouldn't go away easily. Clementine was a typical mistress, just in it for the gifts and free meals. Susanna was a bona fide homewrecker. She wanted to see our marriage end, I could tell by the tone of her text messages."

Carter inwardly chided himself for being so careless with leaving his phone lying around.

"She was in it for keeps, saying how much she loved you and that you two were soul mates. A threat would've done more harm than good since she would just cry about it to you, making me the bad guy.

"I sent a text from your phone saying you were suspicious that I knew about the two of you. You wanted to meet at the cliff around the corner from the café, because you were worried I was following you. I waited for her and watched her step out of the car. She walked over to the edge, admiring the view. Then, I came up behind and…I pushed her over!"

She finished with a sick little smile and hummed the tune of "Oh! Susanna."

Carter backed up slowly, keeping his eyes on Georgia. He thought about the gun in his coat pocket, and tried to think of a reason for going to the hallway to retrieve it without her getting suspicious. She'd killed Susanna, and for all he knew she was planning to kill him.

"Looking back on it, I wish I'd taken care of Clementine the way I did Susanna."

Carter took another step backward.

"Or Sarah…"

"Sarah?" He stopped moving.

"Oh, she's out on the balcony, did I forget to mention that?"

Georgia flipped on the patio lights. Carter stared through the French doors that opened onto the balcony, his mouth agape. There was his girlfriend Sarah, with a black eye and a bloodied rag wrapped over her mouth. She was tied to a chair and teetering very close to the edge of the balcony.

"What the hell did you do to her?" He ran toward the doors.

"I wouldn't open them if I were you!"

Georgia shook her head. He stopped at the doors and his fingers grazed the handles.

"She's tied to the doors," Georgia said, "and I removed the glass panel so she's hovering just over the edge. If you open them, the tautness of the sheets will give and she'll go right over!"

Georgia hummed and tossed the salad with the wooden tongs. Carter looked outside. One of their 500-count Egyptian cotton flat sheets was knotted into a rope and tied to the French doors. The sheet was attached to the chair that held Sarah, and the back legs of the chair were teetering over the edge of the balcony.

"You sick bitch!"

Carter screamed and made a move to open the doors but stopped. He had no idea how long that sheet would hold if Sarah went over. He kept placing his hands on the door handles, then tearing them away.

"Why are you doing this? Can't you just give me a divorce and we'll all move on? Why do you have to hurt Sarah, none of this is her fault!"

"She's a homewrecker! She slept with a married man, and accepted his engagement ring!" Georgia shook her head. "Good thing I got it off her gold-digging fingers already."

She reached into the pocket of her apron and tossed the ring onto the counter. Sparkling against the granite was a five-carat diamond ring.

"That's Sarah's!" Carter shouted.

"And it's ten times nicer than the one you gave me!"

"I was broke then, you know that!"

"And never upgraded my diamond ring like you said you would! No, instead you buy one for this slut!"

Carter released a growl as he grabbed Georgia by the shoulders and shoved her against the wall. A framed photo of the two of them kissing on their wedding day fell to the carpet. He shoved her again, hitting her head against the wall. Her body grew slack in his grip, and he let go of her.

Georgia sank to the carpet next to the wedding photo. He ran to the balcony, still unsure of how to release Sarah. He looked around the doors. There was a window on the left that overlooked the balcony. It was barely big enough to fit Carter.

He grabbed a pewter plant stand and hit it against the window until it broke through the glass. With his elbow he knocked out the jagged pieces that remained in the pane and stepped through. He made his way over to Sarah and gripped the knotted sheet that held her.

"It's going to be okay baby, just hang on!"

The trembling in his voice didn't soothe Sarah. She held her breath and closed her eyes. Carter had one hand around the sheet and gripped her shoulder with his other hand. He pulled her to the middle of the balcony and untied her from the chair. He pulled off the rag covering her mouth and kissed her.

"Thank God you're okay!" Carter said through tears.

"What kind of crazy psycho did you marry? And you said you were separated!"

"I'm sorry, I wasn't totally honest with you."

"Totally honest? You weren't even a tad bit honest!"

"Yes I was! Our marriage has been deteriorating for years."

"Really? Carter, come on! Obviously that's been one-sided if this is your wife's reaction."

"But I do love you, that wasn't a lie!"

Sarah sighed and touched the area near her black eye with a wince. She felt pain all over, although Georgia had only punched her in the face.

Carter put his hand on her shoulder as they stepped inside through the French doors.

"Are you okay?"

"I'll be fine." Sarah shrugged off his hand.

"We should put something cold on that shiner. Wait, what the hell?"

"What?"

"Where is she?" Carter pointed at the wedding photo on the carpet, and Georgia was no longer lying next to it. He bit his lip and glanced over his shoulder.

"Can we please just get out of here?" Sarah walked away from him and into the kitchen.

"Wait a minute! I don't know where she is. She's flipped out Sarah. Look what she did to you!"

"Which is exactly why we should leave!"

Sarah took another step and saw her ring on the counter glinting underneath the tracked lighting. She reached for it, and then heard the sound of breaking glass.

Georgia had thrown a vase at the wall and charged at Carter with a knife. He ran toward the hallway, thinking of the gun in his coat, when Georgia tackled him.

The End of a Marriage

Sarah crouched by the kitchen island and tried to decide if she should step in and stop the fight, or just leave. Carter got the knife out of Georgia's hand and flung it to the floor, then Georgia pushed him and he stumbled toward the French doors, which were still open.

Georgia picked up the knife from the floor and went after him, but she slipped and grabbed his necktie for balance. He tried to shake her off and they struggled as they stumbled toward the part of the balcony missing the glass panel.

Sarah saw what was going to happen and made her way toward the balcony, but they fell over before she could get there. She continued trotting to the balcony, but didn't look over when she heard the horrible splattering sound.

She held back the bile that approached her throat and took several deep breaths. She was trembling, and noticed a Northeastern Huskies sweatshirt hanging over a chair and pulled it on.

Then she caught the glint of her diamond ring under the lights. She walked into the kitchen and picked it up. She chewed on her lip as she mulled over what she should do.

Sarah heard sirens approaching and rushed to the front door, slipping the ring into her pocket. She kept her hands tucked into the sleeves of the sweatshirt so as not to leave any fingerprints on the doorknob.

She left the building as the paramedics were pulling up, fingering the ring as she held back her tears. The ring could help pay for her tuition. She figured it was the least Carter could do.

Newborn

I walked down Teluna Lane. The ice shavings pelted right through my jacket, and the wind felt more like ice than the ice did, but I didn't care. I liked the numbness it brought.

I shouldn't have left Liz in the car, but I just couldn't take it anymore. She was holding Mallory, rocking her back and forth, singing to her and pretending she was still alive. Pretending that her face wasn't blue, that her eyes weren't huge bulges, that her mouth was laughing instead of gaped open like a fish….that her….fuck it. I can't take this.

It was only a couple of months ago that I brought Liz to the hospital, and after six hours of labor, our daughter was born. That was the greatest day of my life, next to the day Liz said "Yes, I'll marry you Harry Watts!" and made me feel like the luckiest guy alive.

It was a running gag with her, to rhyme "I'm gonna marry Harry!" She giggled every time she said that. When she got pregnant last year, after we'd been trying for two years, I thought everything was working out for us.

Then I got laid off, and Liz got a letter in the mail saying there was no need to return to work after her maternity leave because the company was shutting down. Can you fucking believe that? And she worked up 'til two weeks before her due date.

I can thank good ole Bob Newburne for this. That piece of shit would rather close the doors than give up his swank house in the hills. Liz and I worked for Berkshire

Communications for nearly ten years, and this is the thanks we get.

Past Teluna was Crescent Hill, where Bob Newburne and family lived. My feet brought me closer to his house. Liz and I were there two summers ago for a barbeque in his backyard. His wife…hell is her name? Beth? Betty? That's it, Betty. Bob and Betty Newburne, golden couple from college parties and crew matches. They both went to Harvard, both came from money, blond hair and blue eyes, WASP-y types if I ever saw them.

Betty took us on a tour of their house to show off the artwork, antiques displayed in cases, custom-made furniture and a kitchen that was bigger than our bedroom. We planned on getting a bigger place after Mallory was born, but we got evicted instead.

Thought I'd get a job soon enough, no big deal. I'd get a steady paycheck again, we could find a new apartment. But there's nothing out there. Nothing. Everywhere I go, boards up on shop windows. Overgrown lawns on foreclosed homes.

All we had left was the car, luckily it was paid for years ago so no one could take that away. Not exactly the best place to live in, but at least it's some kind of shelter. But it wasn't enough to keep Mallory alive. Not with this winter.

Got to the Newburne house. Their lights were on and the window shades up, I could see inside. It looked so warm, everything looked golden. Then I saw him.

Bob stood by the picture window wearing a fuzzy looking robe and drinking out of a mug. I wanted to pick up a rock and throw it through the window. Wipe that smug look off his face and drop the mug onto the floor. That sonofabitch.

Not sure how long I stood there staring at the house, just stood there until I was numb all over. The lights went out, and I couldn't see inside anymore. Then I thought about Liz, how I'd left her in the backseat rocking Mallory. My heart pumped, feeling came back and I ran to the car.

Liz was so still in the backseat. I was scared. I yanked open the door and sat next to her. She didn't move. She was so cold. I put my arm around her, and placed my palm under her nose. I felt air. Her shoulders heaved, slightly. I relaxed, but just for a second. I had to do something with Mallory.

I tried to pry her out of Liz's arms, and that's when she woke up. She screamed and slapped me, and gripped Mallory.

"We have to bury her, honey." I kept my voice as soft as possible. "We can't keep her here."

"No! I have to keep her warm, she's too cold!" She went back to rocking.

I figured what harm could it do? Let her rock the baby back and forth. She started singing again.

"Hush little Mallory, don't say a word, Mama's gonna buy you a mocking-bird."

That was her go-to song whenever the baby couldn't get to sleep. There was no harm in singing, really, or pretending Mallory's still alive. We're both going down the same path. Pretty soon we'll die of exposure too. Nothing wrong with her living in this fantasy for a bit longer.

I turned on the car to let the heat run, and noticed the gas was running low. We had nothing left to pawn, no money for gas, and just a few packages of cheese crackers in the glove box. I figured it wouldn't be much longer.

I stayed awake all night, kept my arm around Liz who finally drifted off. I kept checking her breathing, half expecting her to drift off in that final way at some point during the night. But I didn't want that. I knew what our fate was, and I wanted us to go through it together.

Maybe I should use the last of the gas in the tank to drive us off that hairpin turn in the mountains. I've often wondered what it would be like, if I made that turn too quickly one day and lost control over the car, and over the edge we went. What a way to go, right? Hell of a lot better than starving and freezing to death out here.

When morning came, the sun reflected off the snow and made everything around the car a blinding whiteness. Liz was asleep and her arms loosened their grip on Mallory. I saw my chance and carefully scooped her up, and covered Liz with a blanket. I stepped out of the car with Mallory in my arms.

I wanted to bury her properly, but the ground was too frozen to dig through with my bare hands. I had to make do with the snow. I brought her over to the big elm tree near the park. There was a crystal clean bank of snow that looked perfect. I knew when the snow melted she'd still be there, and would freak out whoever ended up finding her in the spring, probably start a police investigation. But I also knew that Liz and I would be long gone before then.

I kissed her forehead, and set her down in the snow. She looked so weird, all blue and her face scrunched up, but she still looked as beautiful as she did when she was born. I prayed to God to bring her to a good place, and to bring Liz and me to the same place. I found some comfort in the thought that we'd all be together again soon, and walked back to the car.

Sitting in the driver's seat, I thought about driving us over the cliff while Liz was still asleep. That way she'd die peacefully, and might not even know what was going on until it was too late. I played it out a dozen times in my head, but never turned the key in the ignition. I ate a couple of cheese crackers and kept checking Liz to make sure she was still breathing, and sat there while it was warm in the sun.

When the sun started to fade, Liz stirred under the blanket. I panicked, not wanting to face her when she woke up and realized Mallory wasn't there. I started up the car and drove down Teluna, and when I reached the turn near Crescent Hill something made my hands turn the car onto that road instead of the one that would lead us to the mountains.

I found myself driving near the Newburne house. Dusk was settling in, I could see inside. Bob and Betty were rushing around the house like they were in a hurry. I parked the car in front of the house next door, and a couple minutes later the Newburne's garage door opened and a shiny gray Lexus rolled down the driveway. It passed us, and I glanced inside to see Bob behind the wheel, and Betty in the back as she fussed with a baby in a car seat.

When did they have a baby? Then I remembered. Betty had a baby just before Liz's maternity leave. Bob was talking about it at the office, they had a baby girl…hell is her name? Something with a C or a K. Bob was showing off newborn pictures, but I was too distracted since Liz could go into labor any minute. We had our own newborn on the way and I didn't pay much attention.

I remembered Bob saying our families should get together for birthdays and trips to Chuck E. Cheese since our kids would be the same age. Then that bastard let all of us go, so he could keep this big house in the hills.

"Where's Mallory?" Liz spoke from the backseat. I jumped, thought she was still asleep.

"Where's Mallory? Where is she, Harry?"

She started to rummage around the backseat, as if I had her hidden in the empty cooler.

"Um…" I looked at the Newburne house, imagined how warm it must be inside. I bet they had lots of food, coffee…can't remember the last time we drank coffee. Hell, if we're going to die we might as well get a decent last meal. Even the guys on death row get a meal first.

"She's in there."

I said it before I thought about it, and pointed at the Newburne house. "I brought her in there so she could get warm. Let's go in and get her, okay?"

Liz looked at me, and I knew she didn't believe me. But she also knew that Mallory was dead, and was pretending otherwise. I just wanted inside that house.

"Okay, let's go get her." Liz stepped out of the car, and I followed her. She must still be up for playing pretend. Figured if they caught us and put us in jail, at least we'd be indoors.

I remembered Bob had bragged in the office one day about the house key he'd hidden in the backyard. He thought he was so clever hiding it underneath a fake plastic rock, and the rest of us rolled our eyes when he walked away. Thankfully he still had that hide-a-key contraption. The fake rock was so obvious sitting apart from the garden, right next to the backdoor.

The door opened so easily, I half-expected an alarm to go off, but nothing happened. I brought Liz inside with me, and stopped her when she tried to turn the light switch.

"Let's keep the lights off, okay?"

I grabbed her hand and we went down the hallway. Much of the house was familiar from the barbeque a couple years ago. The end table near the guest bathroom still jutted out and I successfully sideswiped it.

The next hall led to the dining room, and the kitchen beyond that. I pulled Liz behind me and we walked through the dining room and entered the kitchen. Seemed like they redecorated, since the table looked bigger and the cabinets now had glass fronts so you could see the plates and cups inside.

I went straight for the fridge, and the sight of chicken salad, pickles and a gallon of milk almost gave me an orgasm. There was a loaf of bread on the counter, and I grabbed it along with the chicken salad. Liz took some glasses from the cabinet and sat down with me. She munched on a pickle while I spread chicken salad on the bread so fast it tore, but I didn't care. I stuffed my face with everything in front of me, and only took brief reprieves for swigs of milk.

"Slow down, Harry! You'll make yourself sick." She nibbled on a piece of bread and drank some milk.

"I don't care if I get sick, this tastes so damn good! I don't even like chicken salad!"

I started laughing. I don't know why, maybe just giddy from all the food, but I couldn't stop laughing. Liz cracked a smile, and soon joined in with me. It felt so good to be sitting there with her, laughing and eating. It'd been so long since we felt that good. I never wanted it to end.

"Think we could make some coffee?" Liz pointed at a canister on the counter with a label on it that said "Coffee," next to a similar one that said "Decaf."

"Why not?" I thought about looking around to see if ole Bob kept any cigars in the house.

Liz found some filters and started up the coffeemaker. The scent of brewing coffee wafted through the kitchen, one of the greatest smells I could've imagined at that point. I couldn't believe it when I felt myself getting hard, and wondered if Liz would be up for a little romp in Bob and Betty's bed.

The second the coffee was ready we heard a rumbling noise that sounded a lot like a garage door opening. I rushed over to the window and peered out. The shiny gray Lexus was pulling into the driveway.

"Oh my God Harry, we have to get out of here!" Liz put the food back into the fridge and turned off the coffeemaker. But I didn't want to leave. I wasn't ready yet. I thought if we hid out somewhere, they'd go to bed and we could sneak into the kitchen and get that feeling back.

"Harry, come on!"

She grabbed my arm, but I wouldn't move. The garage door closed, I heard footsteps. And the sound of a baby crying.

"Mallory?" Liz let go of my arm. "She's here, Harry, she's here!"

Liz ran out of the kitchen before I could stop her, so I ran after her. Bob and Betty with their baby walked through the door that connected up from the garage. For a few seconds, we all just stood there staring at each other. Then Betty screamed, and the baby's cries grew louder.

"What in the name of God is going on here?" Bob placed his hands on his hips, the same way he did when he reprimanded someone at the office.

"Hi Bob, remember us?" I put my arm around Liz's waist.

"Betty, get the baby upstairs, I'm calling the police!"

I considered letting him do it. At least in jail we'd be warm, have food and could stretch out for sleep. Bob grabbed a cordless phone from the wall and started to dial. Without even thinking about it, my hand flew up and slapped the phone out of his hand.

"You don't remember us, do you? But I guess that's because an asshole like you doesn't give two shits about the people he put out in the street."

"What? I have no idea what you're talking about!"

"Berkshire Comm, you moron. You sold it, you took away both our jobs."

I could hear the baby screeching. Liz turned toward the sound. I grabbed her hand to keep her next to me.

"That doesn't give you any right to break into my home!" Bob reached down to pick up the phone. I let go of Liz's hand and shoved Bob against the wall.

"Unhand me! Unhand me!" Man, he always talked like a douchebag.

"Get out of here, Liz!" I shouted and kept my grip on Bob. Liz left the room.

"Where is she going? What are you doing?"

"This has been a long time coming, ole Bobby Newburne."

I punched him square in his jaw, blood squirted out of his mouth and he doubled over. I never felt so alive. I don't know if it was the food in my belly, the erection bursting through my pants, or doing something I'd wanted to do for years, punch out my boss.

While Bob was trying to catch his breath, I gripped his shoulders and my knee found its way to his face. It hit his nose, and I heard this awful yet satisfying crunching sound. Blood oozed out, and dripped down his face.

Bob fell to his knees clutching his shattered nose. There was a fireplace a few feet away, and resting next to it was an iron poker. I didn't stop and ask myself what I was intending to do. I just did it.

I picked up the poker. Bob was still on his knees, sobbing and bleeding and probably couldn't even see what

Newborn

was coming at him. I held that poker with both hands, thought about the time my dad taught me how to chop wood, how to pick my mark and use the full force of my upper body.

I thought about Mallory, her frozen blue face, and that poker came down just like the axe had that day. My mark was the middle of Bob's head, and just like that day I didn't miss my mark.

I let go of the poker. It was stuck in his head. He fell over and collapsed to the floor, and then the poker twisted and tore out of his skull. He twitched a couple of times and then he was still. I didn't even realize I'd been holding my breath until I let it out, and felt my lungs gasp for air.

A brief thought came into my mind, that Bob wouldn't ever gasp for air again, and I shoved it aside as I ran upstairs to get Liz. We really had to get the hell out of there.

The baby stopped crying, so I had no sound to go by. The upstairs of the Newburne house had a long hallway and many doors that were closed, but one was open.

I walked over to it and stood in the doorway. The room was dark, but I could see the shape of someone.

"Liz? Is that you?" I stepped into the room. It was then I realized it was a nursery. Big crib in the middle of the room with a mobile above it, and Liz was standing next to the crib. She reached down and picked up the baby.

"We found her, Harry! We found Mallory! She's okay, she's okay!" Liz held the baby and half-laughed, half-cried. I didn't know which to do myself.

"Where's Betty?" I had the eerie feeling she'd already called the cops, and we'd be hearing sirens any second.

Liz didn't answer. She rocked the baby back and forth and seemed to be in a different world. The baby cooed and my eyes adjusted to the darkness in the room, and the rest of the nursery came into view. Stuffed bunnies and bears on a dresser, a changing table, a breast pump and on the floor a pair of feet, and then my line of vision centered on the body of Betty Newburne lying on the carpet.

She was perfectly still. Arms splayed out, with a knife sticking out of her chest. I assumed Liz grabbed it from the kitchen.

"Jesus Christ," I whispered, and my voice was hoarse. I was partially relieved that there wouldn't be any sirens approaching, at least not yet. I looked at Liz. She rocked the baby in her arms and had this delirious smile on her face.

"Hush little Mallory, don't say a word, Mama's gonna buy you a mocking-bird. If that mocking-bird don't sing, Mama's gonna buy you a diamond ring."

I fell back against the wall behind me, and sank to the floor across from Betty. Liz was still singing. I didn't have the heart to tell her the baby's name wasn't Mallory, but Clara.

Suddenly everything I knew about the Newburnes came to me: Bob's liking for hot pastrami for lunch, and those goofy Santa ties he wore in December; the greeting cards Betty sent us for every single holiday, even Flag Day; how depressed Bob was when his father passed away, and Betty sewed a mourning patch for him to wear on his sleeve. I always thought that was real classy. The Newburnes had always been a classy pair. Had been…the Newburnes were a "was" now.

Then, for the first time throughout everything, from the lay-offs to living in the car, even Mallory's death, I cried. I looked at little Clara, who had classy parents and a great life ahead of her, now an orphan thanks to us.

I bawled harder than she was bawling, and Liz kept singing. She kept singing, even when sirens could be heard outside, getting louder as they got closer. Betty did call the cops after all, she must've done it before Liz got to her. I tried to get Liz to sneak out through the back door, but she wouldn't budge. When I told her cops were outside, she started singing again. When I tried to take Clara from her, she shrieked and bit my hand.

I leaned over and puked inside the crib. I should've driven us over the cliff at the hairpin turn. At least we'd be in heaven with Mallory. Now we're going to hell.

Jenna Moquin

The Machine

The first thing she sees in the morning is the crack in the ceiling that always leaks when it rains. She remains in bed for a moment, relishing the time before her day begins.

When the cries come from the basinet across the room seconds later, she jolts out of bed. After breastfeeding the baby, she burps her and changes the diaper before placing her back in the basinet.

She twists her long, graying hair into a bun and pulls on a stained but clean housedress. In the narrow hallway she walks past the faded photograph of her wedding day, and the cracked mirror she never looks into.

She reaches the two small rooms that house her eight other children and wakes up the boys before the girls, then goes to the parlor to wake up her husband. He is asleep on the couch, with an empty bottle of whiskey on the floor.

With a soft sigh, she picks up the bottle and tucks it into the apron pocket of her housedress. She whispers in his ear to wake him up. He grunts at her and begins to stretch, and she goes into the kitchen to make breakfast. She places the empty whiskey bottle into the garbage can.

Though she only has five eggs with which to serve nine people, not including herself, she expertly divides them into equally tiny portions. Then she pours cereal into nine mismatched plastic bowls and pours the milk on top.

The Machine

The children arrive in flocks, and her husband follows soon after. They all complain that the cereal is soggy, but eat it anyway. As they eat, she makes nine peanut butter sandwiches and wraps them in brown paper sacks, downing dry handfuls of cereal for her own breakfast while she packs the lunches. After the kids finish eating they line up to take their lunches and leave for school. A few minutes later she hands the last bagged lunch to her husband who leaves for work with a grunt.

She heads into the bedroom to check on the baby, who is sleeping soundly. Soon that baby will join her siblings in the girls' room when the next baby comes. She felt a little sick the other day, and knows another one is coming soon. Sometimes, perhaps all the time, she prays for the day when the great change will come to make her unable to keep having babies.

She sighs and sets off to begin her morning chores. She makes the beds and picks up the dirty clothes from the floor. The hamper is full so it's time to wash the clothes. While she waits for the clothes in the washing machine she cleans the breakfast dishes.

The dryer hasn't worked in some time, so she hangs the wet laundry on a clothesline strung through the kitchen and opens the windows to quicken the process. The house fills with cold air and makes her shiver and wrap a thin robe around herself. At the same time she hears the baby crying, signaling the next feeding.

She picks up the baby and tries not to look at her own hands, cracked and red and rough. She eases into the old wicker rocking chair that is splintering in back. One of the boys found it on the side of the road one day after school. It creaks as she rocks.

Jenna Moquin

The baby nurses hungrily at her breast. She looks down with a grimace, and switches to her other breast. She continues to rock back and forth for a while after the baby is done feeding. This is the only time besides bedtime when she can sit back and somewhat relax, though it is bittersweet as her nipples become sore.

When these times come she likes to pretend she is someone else, someone who doesn't have eight children, a newborn baby and another on the way.

On the days when she goes to the market, she sees people on the glossy covers of magazines while she waits in line at the checkout. She has never been able to afford one of those magazines, but she enjoys reading the titles on the covers and looking at the pretty, fancy people in the photographs.

She imagines they have people working for them, washing their clothes, cleaning their dirty dishes and floors. They probably wear fluffy bathrobes and slippers, and eat steak every night. She doesn't usually see their hands in the pictures on the magazine covers, but she imagines their hands are soft and smooth, not cracked and red and dry.

With a sigh she tears herself out of the rocking chair. She places the baby back in the basinet, and continues with her chores.

She cleans the floors and spends extra time in the kitchen where it is most needed. The frying pan had been soaking since breakfast, and she scrubs it clean along with a few stray cups and plates she'd found strewn around the house. She finishes the dishes and dries them with a towel as thin and faded as her robe. When she opens the bottom cabinet to put the frying pan away, she sees the whiskey bottle hiding behind the cooking oil.

The Machine

She knows that if her husband didn't drink so much, they could probably afford more food. But she also knows what happens when she says things like that out loud. She still has the scars on the backs of her hands.

As she wipes the countertops her eyes move toward her hands. Her nails are thin and ragged from scraping at stains on clothes and dishes. They have a pinkish tint, as the puffy skin underneath shines through. Her gaze wanders to her cracked red knuckles, and then the burn scars.

The day she spoke to her husband about cutting back on whiskey, he picked up the frying pan she'd been using to cook their breakfast eggs, and rested it on top of her hands. He did it so deftly and calmly, he kept the eggs neatly in the pan, so as not to ruin the food. He served breakfast to the children while she cried softly in the bathroom and bandaged her hands.

Shaking her head out of the memory, she feels the clothes on the line to see if they are dry. They're slightly damp, but she takes them down and folds them anyway so she can close the windows.

After she puts the clothes away, she hears the baby's cries. She relishes in the chance to sit down for a moment, and rocks her back to sleep. She dozes off for a moment herself.

Before it's time for the children to arrive home from school, she walks around the one-story home and surveys her cleaning for the day. She passes the table in the hallway that houses the children's school photos. There are so many there isn't any space left on the table. She sighs and turns away from them.

Soon after the children arrive home, she begins the preparations for dinner. She pulls out two boxes of pasta, and takes out the plates to set the table. Two of them have a floral pattern along the edges, four of them are plain white plates, and the rest are from an old wedding china set she found at a yard sale.

She fills up the largest pot with water and sets it on the stove to boil, and calls to the children to wash up for dinner. Tonight they are having pasta with butter and salt, and one slice of bread each.

She places a handful of cooked pasta from the strainer into a plastic container, and places it aside for herself later.

The children enter the kitchen and sit at the table. They begin eating as soon as she hands them slices of bread. The front door opens and the unmistakable grunt of her husband follows. He slams the door behind him and stomps into the kitchen.

She holds her breath as he walks in. The first thing he does is head for the bottom cabinet. He reaches behind the cooking oil to retrieve the whiskey bottle, he glances her way and she glances away. He takes a long swig from it.

He sits at the table without saying a word to anyone and eats his dinner. The children finish eating, and the boys ask if they can go outside to play. She grants them permission, but tells them to be home as soon as the streetlights come on.

As her husband finishes eating, she takes the children's plates away to soak in the sink. He gets up from the table and stands behind her, rubbing her backside, the usual indication that he wants to take a trip to the bedroom.

She obediently turns around and lets him kiss her and pinch her sore nipples, and follows him into the bedroom. She undresses and lies down on the bed with her legs open.

He removes only his pants, and mounts her. As soon as he enters her, she squeezes her eyes shut and bites down on her bottom lip. After he finishes with a grunt, he rolls

The Machine

away from her, puts his pants back on and leaves the room. She is relieved that the baby didn't wake up, but there wasn't much noise to wake her up anyway.

Her husband grabs the whiskey bottle from the kitchen. He goes to the parlor and turns on the radio. An announcer's relaying of a baseball game can be heard. He lies down on the couch cradling the bottle.

She gets up from bed and sighs as she pulls on her robe. Her body aches with nearly every move. In the kitchen she pulls out her cold dinner and digs into the pasta. She eats the small portion quickly with her eyes on the door.

She goes to the parlor to check on her husband, and he is already snoring. He stopped sleeping in their bedroom once the new baby came, and she is grateful for that.

The baby cries, and she rushes to feed her. When the streetlights begin to come on she goes to the front door, opens it halfway and calls for the boys to come inside.

After finishing the dishes and wiping down the table, she rounds up the children and tells them to brush their teeth. She sends them to their rooms where she knows several of them will stay up for a while, but she doesn't care as long as they are quiet.

She goes throughout the house and makes sure the doors and windows are locked. Back in her bedroom, the baby is sleeping deeply and she tucks a blanket around her. She puts on a once-white nightgown and lets her hair down before she climbs into bed.

She stares up at the crack in the ceiling as the beginning feelings of sleep overcome her. She relishes in the few moments of serenity she has before her body shuts down for the night, only to get up in a few hours to do it all over again.

Office Politics

"I killed a man once." Katie took a drag from her cigarette and sat back on Scott's sofa. Scott had been pouring merlot into her wineglass, but stopped when she spoke.

"Come again? I thought we were just having drinks tonight, not true confessions."

Katie giggled and hiccoughed. She stamped out her cigarette on the crystal ashtray atop the coffee table and took a sip of wine.

"It's the alcohol. It always turns into a truth serum for me. It's why I typically drink alone."

"So is this like you killed a man for real, or one of those mind games where you killed his spirit, or something?"

"For real. Want to hear about it?"

Katie unbuttoned the top of her silk blouse and kicked off her maddeningly uncomfortable high heels. She tucked her legs underneath her skirt and rested her elbow against the back of the sofa.

Scott looked at her lush brown hair that framed her face which held a mischievous smile. He decided she was playing with him, and thought he'd play along.

"Okay, I'll bite. Tell me all about it." He poured himself some wine.

"First of all, the Katie you know, marketing director with a corner office, she didn't come from money."

"Oh?"

"My parents weren't destitute, but we weren't comfortable by any stretch. They both worked two jobs, and we, my brother and sisters, rarely saw them together. We had this really small place. It was an old colonial home that had been sectioned off into a bunch of apartments, and ours was on the first floor. All four girls shared one bedroom, with only two beds. Our room was connected to the master bedroom, and we had to walk through Mom and Dad's room to get anywhere else in the house. Mickey, my brother, he had a large closet for his room with just a cot inside."

"Wow. I'm even more impressed that you've made it this far in life."

"Amazing what a gymnastics scholarship can do. Anyway, one day when I was thirteen, I was home by myself on a Saturday, which was pretty rare. My dad was working his part-time job at the laundry place, and my mom had taken Mickey to the doctor. He was always getting sick, allergic to everything. I think my sisters were at friend's houses, probably all trying to get time away from the family like I was enjoying. Sharing such a small space with so many people can take its toll on you."

"I can only imagine. I had one sister who was ten years older than me, and she was off to college when I was a kid. For a while, we had two spare bedrooms in my house."

"Spoiled brat!" Katie tapped his shoulder and laughed. Scott laughed with her, and refreshed her drink.

"Please, continue."

"That day I remember thinking how nice it would be to finally have a bed all to myself. Take a nap and spread out, something I never got to do. I climbed into bed, and I'm not sure how long I was asleep but it felt like a while. Then I woke up to these strange noises."

"What kind of noises?"

"I heard doors opening and closing, creaking floorboards, and a weird clanging noise, like keys jingling. So I got up and walked into my parents' room, and it was a mess. My mother's jewelry box was on the floor, empty. The closet was opened and clothes had been tossed out and thrown onto the bed and floor. I didn't know what was going on. I went into the hallway and didn't see anything. The noises I'd heard had stopped, and I walked into the kitchen. That was when I saw him."

At first Scott had thought Katie was fooling around with him. Then he looked into her eyes and saw such a faraway look he realized she was deep in the throes of a memory.

"He wasn't very tall, and he was thin and frail-looking. He had a mustache with crumbs in it, and he was holding a box of crackers. There were crumbs all over the table, along with shopping bags full of our food, and a Ziploc bag that had my mom's jewelry inside of it. I stared at him, and at the bags, and that's when he put down the crackers and pulled out a switchblade. I turned to run out of the kitchen, but he grabbed me."

Scott's eyes had widened into saucers, and he stared at Katie with his chin in his hands, the wine forgotten. The jazz that had been coming out of his speakers stopped, and he didn't get up to change the music.

"He covered my mouth and I tried to bite his hand. He dragged me to the pantry, and set down the switchblade on a bag of potatoes. He still had my mouth covered, and even though he wasn't a big guy he was still bigger than me, and easily pinned me to the shelves. I struggled, my arms tried to reach up to his face to scratch him, but he held me back at arm's length. With his other hand, he started to unbutton his pants."

She took a sip of wine and continued.

"I started to cry, and pray that someone, my dad, sisters, anyone, would come home right at that second. I was so sorry for ever feeling happy to have the house to myself that day."

Katie wiped her hand underneath her eyes, and Scott gave her a tissue. She thanked him and blew her nose, and he poured more wine for both of them.

"I haven't talked about that day in years, but it feels like it was yesterday. I remember staring at the switchblade on the potatoes, the way it shined from the sun coming into the pantry. He was still struggling with his pants. He glanced down and his grip on me loosened. I stared at the knife on the potatoes, and the way it shined. I knew if I could just get to that knife, I could stop him. If I had that knife in my hands, I could make it all stop.

"He was having trouble getting his pants undone with only one hand, and took his other hand away, probably thinking it would only be for a second. But that second was all I needed. I grabbed the knife and didn't even look before I turned around and stuck it in him. It went into his stomach. His pants had come undone and were around his ankles. He had this tiny little penis that was still hard when I stabbed him. He looked at me, then down at the knife, and he tried to pull it out but he only succeeded in making himself bleed more. Blood was pouring down his legs and into his socks and pants, and I just stood there."

Scott had been taking a sip of his wine, but at the mention of blood, he stopped with a grimace. He set down his glass of merlot and looked at Katie. She still had that faraway look in her eyes, and a sole tear went down her cheek. He caught the tear with his finger before it reached her chin, and wiped it away.

Katie grabbed his hand, and clutched it so tightly he felt his knuckles crack.

"What the hell?" Scott said.

Katie didn't answer, but she dropped his hand and stood up from the sofa. She traipsed across the carpet to the bay window that overlooked Central Park.

"Remember the Central Park Jogger? The woman who was raped in the park back in the eighties?"

"Um, yeah…" Scott glanced at the clock on the wall. He wondered if he still had time in the evening to find a new date at the club.

"I sometimes wonder what was going through her mind when it happened. When that guy held me down in the pantry, before I focused on the knife, I knew he was going to rape me. And I thought about where I would have to go when it happened. Where my mind would have to go, that is. I thought it would be the time my parents took us to Six Flags when they got a bunch of coupons for the park, or the time my sisters and I stayed up all night on Halloween watching scary movies and sharing our candy.

"I couldn't decide between the two, and that was when the knife became the only thing I could see. I was so happy the sun shined on the knife the way it did. So happy that I didn't already go off to Six Flags or Halloween, because if I had I don't know if the knife would've been so clear to me. I wonder if the Central Park Jogger did that when it happened. If she went somewhere in her mind, some place that always made her happy."

Scott sighed into his hands, and glanced at the clock again.

"Listen Katie, it was awful what happened to that jogger, and what happened to you. Truly awful. But you should feel grateful that you stopped it from happening, and didn't suffer the same fate as that jogger."

"No, I only took a man's life. Yeah, I'm really grateful for that."

Scott made no effort to conceal his next sigh. He then stormed over to the wine rack with a grunt, but instead of retrieving a bottle he opened the top of the rack that held a cubby drawer. He pulled out a black leather valet and carried it to the sofa.

"Mind if I turn this back into a party?" Scott opened the valet and inside lay a glass vial half-filled with white crystalline powder, a small mirror and a larger glass vial filled with red, blue and yellow tablets.

"Coke?" Katie eyed the powder that Scott shook out of the vial onto the mirror. He scraped it into thin lines with an Ace of Spades card.

"I've got some uppers and downers too." Scott pointed at the vial of pills. "For you, I'd recommend the uppers."

Katie watched as he snorted a line of cocaine, followed by a second one in the other nostril.

"I told you about my…my experience tonight. I told you about it because I thought we were close. I thought it was something you'd understand, and could handle."

"Katie baby, of course I can handle it, but come on, it's Friday night! We both had a long week at the office, and I thought tonight we'd have some wine, have a little private party of our own…"

Scott patted the seat next to him and winked at her.

"I'm really not in the mood anymore."

Katie walked over to the sofa, reached down and picked up her heels. She placed them on her feet and buttoned her blouse.

"Are you kidding me right now?" Scott raised his eyebrows.

"No. And by the way, I hate coke. It turns people into assholes."

Katie turned and walked to the door, and grabbed her blazer and purse on the way. Before she reached the door, Scott rushed up behind her and slammed the wall with his palm. She turned around with a start, and saw a Scott she'd never seen before. His eyes were wild, and his pupils were pinpoints.

"You'd better watch what you say to me. Don't forget who put you in the position you have now. I can take it away just as easily."

"No you can't, you'd have to go to the board. I know how it works."

"Then I'll just have to tell them that little story you told me tonight. How you killed a man when you were just a kid. I think the duties of the marketing director will affect your mental health. It's a stressful position, Katie, and I'm not so sure I have the confidence that you'll be able to handle it."

"What?"

"I'm only thinking about what's best for the company." Scott folded his arms across his chest.

"You're serious? Please, Scott, I just watched you bump cocaine!"

"That's your word against mine. Even if they drug test me, this stuff will be out of my system by Monday. But I'm quite sure there are county records about what you did when you were a kid. Unless you buried the body and never told a soul until now."

Office Politics

"The police were involved, but it was self-defense so I was absolved. My record is clear, nothing to hide."

"That doesn't mean your reputation would be clear."

Katie stared at him and bit her lip. Scott opened the door and she stepped into the hallway. The door slammed behind her, and with a steady gait, she walked to the elevator.

Inside the elevator, as Katie descended toward the lobby, she pulled out her phone and looked at her reflection in the mirrored doors.

"Isn't possession of cocaine a felony?" She asked herself with a smirk.

The doors opened to the lobby and Katie walked out of the building. While she made a call to the local police station, she mentally redecorated Scott's office for herself.

The Heaven or Hell Line

Dale looked down at his hands. There were no scratches, no blood, but he'd felt them go through the windshield along with the rest of him when the car hit the guardrail. He hadn't been wearing his seatbelt and when the impact came he'd flown straight through the glass. But he wasn't in pain, and didn't see any glass fragments, thought he couldn't see much of anything due to the blindingly bright light that surrounded him.

He sniffed the air. He thought with a car crash that the scent of gasoline would be present, but the air had this wonderful sweet aroma that reminded him of summer days as a child. Something mixed with freshly mown lawns and the ocean. It was the scent of warm sun hitting everything around, the scent of sun-kissed leaves and grass, the scent of summer. He suddenly felt wonderful all over, but then it hit him that Julie had been in the car with him.

"Julie!" He shouted, and tried to look for her through the brilliant light. He started to move forward, but then realized he couldn't feel his legs. He couldn't feel them, or his arms, or the rest of his body. He tried not to think about it and focused on making sure his wife was safe.

"Julie! Are you okay? Where are you?"

He had a sinking feeling that she wasn't answering because she was unconscious, or dead. He brushed the thought aside and called for her again.

"Julie, please answer me!"

"Hey, calm down over there," said a man's voice to Dale's left. "No need to shout."

"We were in an accident," Dale said to the voice. "Please, help us!"

"I know, I know, we're all dead here. But calm down will you?"

"Easy for you to say," said a woman's voice to Dale's right. "You knew you were gonna die for months with your brain tumor!"

"So what? He still don't need to yell that loud."

"Some meet an untimely death, just keep that in mind Buddy."

"Oh bite me, Angie."

Dale couldn't see them but he could hear them. There were at least two voices, possibly three. He hoped someone was helping his wife.

"Julie!" He tried to run his tongue along the bottom part of his teeth, the way he always did when he was nervous. There was a glimmer of feeling and then he couldn't feel much of anything. He wasn't in pain, and some moments he felt numb all over. He felt remnants of limbs every few seconds and then they'd vanish. It was like his body was only elusively there.

The only things that seemed to be working properly were his voice, ears and nose. His hopeful assumption was that it was shock, not that he was blind and paralyzed, and he tried to squash the image of his life in a wheelchair with Julie dead. He felt the urge to vomit, but it passed. Or, he just couldn't feel it anymore.

"Why won't anyone tell me what's going on? Where is Julie? Julie!"

Dale was so afraid she was dead. She wasn't answering him, and everyone around him was acting so strangely. As if they were trying to figure out how to tell this poor man that his wife was mangled in the car wreck. He began to cry.

"Will someone set this guy straight so he'll shut up?" Buddy shouted.

"I'll have to do it of course, since you won't," Angie said.

"What do you want from me?" Buddy said. "My wife is now a widow, you think that makes me happy?"

Dale could hear other people farther away, sounding just as distraught as he was. He assumed they were also victims of the same accident, and wondered how many other cars were involved.

A woman's voice howled out the name "Marco!" over and over. Perhaps to try and lighten the mood, a voice nearby said "Polo!" softly, and a couple of chuckles ensued a few feet away.

Suddenly Dale felt the atmosphere around him shift, and there was a slight tingling sensation down his back.

"My name's Angie. I'll explain what's happened to you."

He recognized the woman's voice from earlier.

"Oh thank you! My wife and I were in an accident. I don't know how many other cars were involved, how many others were hurt. But I'm so worried because she's not answering me, and…and…I can't…I can't see! And I can't feel my legs, or my arms, or anything!"

Angie sighed.

"What's your name?"

"Dale."

"Nice to meet you, Dale. Listen, you can't feel anything because you no longer have a body. You're just a soul. And you can't see anything because your soul hasn't accepted what's happened to you yet."

"What?"

"I'm sorry to be the one to tell you this, but you're dead."

"What?"

"You're dead." Angie raised her voice. "I don't know if your wife is dead too, but you are because you're here. This is the Heaven or Hell Line."

"The...the what?" Dale was starting to have hope that this was just some strange, vivid dream.

"This is the line to the pearly gates," Angie continued. "Saint Peter is up there judging everyone. This is where he'll decide if you get to go to Heaven, or have to go to Hell."

"Angie..." Buddy said. "Be careful. You don't want to scare another one."

"Quiet down Buddy. This poor guy needs some answers. Looks like it'll be a long wait anyway."

"What?" Dale knew none of this could be real. He knew it had to be a dream. He desperately wanted to wake up and see Julie's face smiling at him.

"You sure this guy isn't just hard of hearing?" Buddy said.

"Hearing I've got," Dale said. "Some other senses seem to be gone."

"They'll come and go," Angie said. "That's what it's like here. This is where you find out what's going to happen to you in the afterlife, and it's sort of like limbo. There's a chance your wife is here too. No guarantees, but you never know. My husband Luke and I have gone through several lives together."

"Several lives? You mean like, reincarnation?"

"Yes, and it follows the laws of karma. As long as you do right in life you get a new life, if that's what you choose. You can either stay in Heaven, or be reincarnated. When I get up there and pick my next life, I'll leave a note with Saint Peter to tell Luke where I am so he can pick his new life close to me. That way we can find each other again. Luke is my soul mate, though he's had different names in his different lives, same as me. But we call each other our soul names, right Buddy?"

"Right. That's one of those things in life you can't control, what name you're given. Same as you have no control over where you grow up, or who your parents are. But if you learn to play this game, you can control that. You can choose where your new life will take place, same way you can choose to change your name when you get older."

"Wait, you can choose that stuff?"

"As long as you do right," Angie said. "You have to be a good person in order to do what Buddy and Luke and I do."

"Exactly," Buddy said. "You can't be an asshole and get to choose your next life. You're an asshole and kill somebody, Saint Peter chooses where you get your next chance to redeem yourself."

"And it's usually something ironic, like whatever bad thing you did, ends up happening to you. You murder someone in cold blood, in your next life you'll be murdered."

"He certainly has a great sense of humor." Buddy chuckled.

"And so on and so on until you get your full set of chances."

"How many chances do you get?" Dale asked.

"Seven," Angie and Buddy said in unison.

"And after the last chance, if you didn't right your wrongs, you go to Hell?"

"Yup," they both said.

"But wait!" Dale started to panic. "How do I know this wasn't my last chance?"

"That's something Saint Peter would know," Angie said. "We can't answer that for you. You'll find out when you get up there."

"I doubt it was your last chance," Buddy said. "You'd remember at least a couple of lives."

"And you wouldn't have been so frantic when you first got here!"

"Exactly," Buddy said. "Life is just one big roller coaster, and you'll see it that way the more lives you live. If you realize it's just a ride, you won't get so bummed out when shit happens. Because that's one of the things you can always count on in life, shit will happen. That's the dip in the roller coaster when your stomach drops. Your dad has cancer; your kid got suspended; you lost your job; you slept with *that* girl from the bar. That's the stuff you can't control in life, but if you realize it's just part of the ride, dealing with it ain't so bad because there's the good stuff too. Your kid hit a homerun; your dad was on *Jeopardy;* you got a new job; *that* girl gave you her number!"

Dale thought about Julie, as she had been *that* girl for him. His father had always told him there were four quintessential moments in a man's life: losing his virginity, getting married, becoming a father, and having the right woman smile at you. Julie had been that woman for him. She was the most beautiful girl he'd ever seen.

It was their Romantic Poetry class, and they were reading Percy Bysshe Shelley. He caught her eye over her notebook and she smiled at him while biting her lip. He loved that.

After class, he asked her what she thought of *Love's Philosophy* and when she said "I loved it," he almost melted. Her voice was smooth, chocolatey and sensual. Listening to her speak made him feel like he was indulging in some sort of guilty pleasure. He desperately wanted to kiss her, and made a point to find out her schedule so he could show up whenever she was walking out of class.

Dale was so enraptured in his memories of those first few months with Julie that he didn't notice the line around him coming into focus. The bright light thinned and faded and he could suddenly see things more clearly. He was getting closer to the top of the line, and Saint Peter.

He followed the movement around him as the line pushed forward, lost in his reverie, feeling drowsy. It was easy to drift in and out of memories in this place. He thought if this were indeed limbo, then that perhaps made sense. He still hoped he was in a vivid dream and would hear Julie's voice any minute telling him to wake up, but it was waning with his acceptance of what had happened to him. He assumed that was also why his vision was coming into focus, as Angie had said it would.

When it was his turn at the top of the line he could see Saint Peter. He sat behind a window that resembled a bank teller's and was flanked by white partitions trimmed in gold. He had a long, twirling mustache and thinning beard that reached below his belt. He also had matched luggage under his eyes. He yawned and waved at Dale to approach.

"Hello, I was told you could give me some answers?"

"Oh boy, another newbie," Saint Peter said while rolling his eyes. "Just what I need! Listen, you died, this is the Heaven or Hell Line."

The Heaven or Hell Line

"I know, somebody already told me that. But I don't know what I'm supposed to do."

Saint Peter sighed and spoke in a low monotone, as if he'd repeated this line several times.

"The laws of karma are simple and finite. Those who do wrongly in life do not have a choice in the afterlife. They are sent back to a new life, where they pay for the wrongs they did in the previous life, and so on and so on."

"That's what Angie said. So the Buddhists and Hindus were pretty much right all along, then."

"Sort of…" Saint Peter tapped his fingers and looked at his watch. "It's like a mix of religions. We try to keep it as even as possible. Those who learn from their mistakes can either go on to Heaven, or keep going on in new lives. Some have been doing this for hundreds of years. They enjoy the roller coaster of life so much, 'the ride,' as some call it, that they want to keep on riding."

"And that's okay?"

"Of course, have fun with it! Being a soul is a great thing, as long as you take care of yourself and treat others well. Do unto others as you would have them do unto you, and all that. We're not the fire and brimstone that the old Puritans would've had you believe. Each soul gets seven chances to get it right. If they don't learn the lessons from the life where they did wrong, they get another chance, and so on until they learn. Seven chances, before they are sent to Hell."

"Can you tell me, what is Hell like?"

"In Hell, the soul relives the wrongs they did in life, for eternity. Some lives on Earth are just like that, people making the same mistakes in a vicious cycle. I see it all the time."

"What about me? How many lives have I had?"

"Let's check." Saint Peter waved his hand. A tablet with a white leather cover appeared in mid-air and hovered while he scrolled with his forefinger.

"Damned search function isn't working again. Apple will be the death of me, I tell you. When Steve Jobs died he decided to stay here but his software still needs updates every five seconds!"

"Steve Jobs?"

"Yes. His soul had been around for centuries. He didn't want to keep playing, so he's just hanging out up here. Ah!"

He stopped scrolling.

"Here were are. Dale Aldous Rutherford. Interesting, looks like this was your second life."

"Second life? How would I have known that?"

"You wouldn't have. You typically only remember when you get here."

"But I don't remember having a first life!"

"Interesting…let's see…"

He scrolled down the screen of the floating tablet.

"What bad luck, eh? You also met an untimely death in your former life, poor soul."

"I did?"

"Yes, you died in your sleep as an infant, you were only three months old. So you wouldn't have remembered that!"

"I lost two chances and didn't even know it. That's not fair!"

"No no no, it's *life* that isn't fair. The afterlife is quite fair. See, when you meet an untimely death it's a freebie. It doesn't count toward the official seven chances."

"Oh, I see. I can't believe I died as a baby in my first life."

"And in your next life you died at age thirty-six in a car accident. Drunk driver rammed you into a guardrail. And he, of course, is still alive. Funny how that always happens, isn't it?"

"What about my wife? Did she live?"

"Let's see…hmmm….yes, she survived the accident."

"Oh thank God!"

"She's quite devastated over your death."

Dale sighed. He was happy that Julie was still alive, but sad that it meant they wouldn't be together any time soon. They couldn't embark on a new life together like Angie and her husband.

"Wait a second," Saint Peter said while he tapped at the floating tablet. "I just got an urgent email from God…ha, lucky break for you!"

"What is it?"

"God said, since you met two untimely deaths for your first two lives, and you seem like a nice fellow, we're going to give you the choice early on."

"What do you mean?"

"Usually you'd have to go through seven lives until you got the choice to stay in Heaven, but since you met two untimely deaths we're giving you the choice now. You can either be reincarnated, or stay here. You don't have to keep playing if you don't want to. So what do you want to do?"

"I'm not sure. Can I have a minute to think it over?"

Saint Peter sighed and rolled his eyes.

"I suppose, but be quick about it. I have a lot of work to do today."

He closed his window with a little grate and a sign appeared from above that said "Back in a minute!" On the sign was a hand-drawn angel flying away, its wings surrounded by smoke.

Dale looked around at the other souls waiting in line. He felt like he'd been in that line for a very long time, but also felt like only moments had passed.

The only place he wanted to be was with Julie, but he couldn't be with her anymore. He liked this place, with the summery scent in the air, and its way of shifting him into memories and making them feel real. This place could make an eternity feel like a long weekend.

He knocked on the grate.

"Yes?" Saint Peter opened it. He had a cup of coffee in his hand.

"If I decide to stay in Heaven, would I get to see Julie, look over her?"

"Yes."

"And if I decide later on that I want to be reincarnated, can I still do that?"

"Yes…" Saint Peter sighed and tapped his fingers.

"Then I'm going to stay. I'll wait for Julie, and when she gets here we can start a new life together like Angie and Luke!"

"I see, you want to leave a note for your wife when she gets here?"

"No, I'll stay here and give you a hand. You look like you could use some help! This line is pretty long, and I have a feeling it never gets small."

"Wait, what?" Saint Peter's eyes widened.

"Seems like you could use an extra hand, and all I want to do is wait for my wife. If I'm here manning the gates with you, then I'll be sure to catch her as soon as she gets here!"

"Are you sure?" Saint Peter didn't bother trying to hide the gratitude in his voice. He unlocked the door that separated him from the line, and Dale stepped inside. Saint Peter shook his hand.

"You'll have to train me of course, but I'm a quick study."

"No problem!"

Saint Peter smiled, for the first time since Dale met him.

"Here, let me show you around!" He motioned for Dale to follow him.

"First I'll show you the break room, that Keurig machine's a little finicky."

Dale followed him down a narrow hallway that was as blindingly bright as the rest of the place. Saint Peter stopped before they reached the end of the hallway and turned around to face him.

"I'll also let you in on the Heaven or Hell line."

"I thought I was just in that line?"

"No, not the line of people waiting out there. The line we tell people. There's no place called Heaven, or Hell. They don't exist the way the religions say. They couldn't, actually. It's impossible for Heaven and Hell to exist as actual places, because everyone's version of them would be different. The only afterlife is reincarnation."

"But what about everything you just told me, the seven chances at life and all that stuff?"

"We tell people they have seven chances to get into Heaven to make them act like better people. The afterlife of Heaven or Hell is just a line to get people to stop acting like jerks."

"But what happens when people reach the seven chances and choose to stay in Heaven?"

"We zap their memories and send them back to Earth, and give them great lives with happiness and luck and all that. That's Heaven on Earth. If they're supposed to go to

Hell, we give them miserable lives and they relive their wrongs over and over. That's Hell on Earth."

"But what about Steve Jobs? You said he was here?"

"Oh he's just hanging out with God, his quarters could be classified as a 'Heaven' of sorts, I suppose. The buffets, the spas, the bedsheets...you should see the fish tank he's got back there! But if you ask me, God's a little too attached to his iPhone."

"So if I had decided to stay in Heaven, but not helped you out here, you would've reincarnated me?"

"Yes..." Saint Peter looked sheepish. "Sorry, that's what we do. But you would've had an awesome life!"

Dale gave him a half-smile.

"We only let a select few in on the Heaven or Hell line, you know." Saint Peter winked at him.

"I have to admit, it is a great line."

"It's okay, I guess."

"Well, what lines do you like?"

Saint Peter furrowed his eyebrows, then his face lit up and he looked at Dale with a smirk.

"I think this is the beginning of a beautiful friendship."

Dale chuckled and Saint Peter put his arm around him as they walked into the break room together.

Dug Out

The dirt caked underneath my fingernails as I tried to dig Connie out. She was buried up to her bare shoulders and I could see her tan line, a little white spaghetti strap from her bikini. She was still breathing, that much I could tell, and her eyes were open, but she wasn't seeing me.

Trying to dig out someone with your bare hands is fucking hard. A couple of my nail tips ripped off already, but I don't care. I have to get her out of there. I don't know where her dad is, and I don't know when he's coming back.

"Connie! Connie! Wake up, it's Marissa!"

I thought about slapping her to see if it would snap her out of it.

"What did he do to you?"

My voice cracked. And then my cheeks were wet. I knew I shouldn't have let her come here alone. She was just going to pick up a few things, and then we were going to leave for Boston and never think about this stupid hick town again. I brushed away the tears and kept digging. I could see the top of her boobs where that adorable little mole was on her upper right one. Then I saw a tiny ant crawl over it and gagged, but didn't stop digging.

Bugs were probably crawling all over her, worms and ants and who knows what else. I couldn't stop myself from picturing bugs crawling all over her boobs, her clit, her lips, even crawling inside her pussy. I didn't want to answer the question a voice inside me kept asking: would I still be able to eat her out knowing that the worms were crawling in and out?

I felt myself about to get sick and clamped my mouth shut and breathed through my nose, the way I always do to keep myself from throwing up. I just pretend there's a lock on my mouth, and concentrate on something else. It's worked every time I got too drunk and every time I got the flu.

Focusing too much on the task at hand wasn't helping. I kept thinking about worms crawling in and out of her. I made myself think about happier times between us, like the first time I won her a teddy bear playing Whack-a-Mole, and the first time we kissed. That brought me back to how we got started in the first place.

Connie and I have been friends for as long as I can remember. We sat next to each other in Mrs. Greenfield's class second grade, and again in Mr. Hennesy's class fifth grade. But it wasn't until junior high that we realized how we really felt about each other.

I was always a tomboy, played softball and field hockey and had more fun hanging out with boys. But the thought of kissing them made me uncomfortable.

I thought maybe I just wasn't ready, and that I would be one day whenever I got married. But that day was a long way off, so I concentrated on school, sports and having fun with my friend Connie, the girl I liked hanging out with more than any other girl at school. I guess you could say we were best friends, but we never called each other anything lame and co-dependent like that.

Connie was more girly than a tomboy, but in other ways she was a lot like me. We liked the same movies and music, and she didn't like the thought of kissing boys either.

Dug Out

We thought we'd try practicing on each other to see how it went, and one day we tried kissing in her bedroom.

The first time we kissed felt like Fourth of July, Christmas, and a trip to Canobie Lake all rolled into one. Connie said she saw stars in the sky even though it was the middle of the day. I remember thinking if that's what kissing was like, I was ready to start kissing boys.

So we went on a double date with two boys from the baseball team. They were both really cute, and sweet, and we had fun getting pizza and then going to the batting cages. But at the end of the date, when I kissed him, it didn't feel the same as it did with Connie. When we talked about it over the phone later that night, she said the same thing happened to her.

"Are we lesbians, or something?" I said with a laugh.

"I just know I would rather kiss you than any other boy I've seen."

When she said that, I got tingles all over. I wanted to kiss her again, kiss places besides her face, kiss every part of her body.

Connie was more into trying boys again than I was, but I went along with it for her sake. We tried a couple more double dates, and Connie even went as far as giving a boy a blow job but I couldn't make it that far. When she went down on me for the first time, she said it was a thousand times better than when she went down on the boy.

One time after my softball practice we went into the dugout and hid until everyone left. Then we made out and took turns eating each other out for hours and hours. Connie said it gave new meaning to the phrase "nappy dugout." I love her for saying stuff like that.

Just after Connie's eighteenth birthday last week, she decided to come out to her parents. I warned her about it, since her dad is one of those people who thinks women and anyone who isn't white are beneath him. Those people cannot be reasoned with. But she insisted on being up front with her parents, and we were moving in together no matter what they said. We already paid first and last month's rent, and have enough saved to get by for the next couple months while we look for jobs.

I didn't have the same parental problems as Connie since mine died when I was a baby. My grandmother raised me and I did come out to her, but she's always been so indifferent toward me I don't know if she was happy for me or happy that *Wheel of Fortune* was coming on. She never seemed to notice how often Connie stayed over, in my room, sometimes for days on end. If she did, she never said anything about it.

Connie's dad didn't take it so well, as suspected. He started running around the house screaming and swearing. Her mother didn't say anything, just went into the kitchen and started doing the dishes while she hummed to herself. Her dad went into the backyard and slammed the door on his way out, and then we heard the sounds of glass breaking. I got up and looked through the window. He was throwing beer bottles at the cemented patio. I shook my head at Connie. She stayed at my place that night.

When Connie said she was coming here to pick up some things she wanted to bring to the new place, I had a bad feeling. When she didn't meet me at the coffee shop afterward, I got really worried so I came over to the house.

The car was in the garage, but no one answered when I knocked. The door was unlocked so I walked inside. The television was on, but no one was watching it. I called "Hello!" a couple of times but no answer. I turned to walk upstairs to Connie's room, and noticed the basement door

Dug Out

was open. I thought maybe Connie was down there looking for boxes, and just didn't hear me when I called out.

I walked through the kitchen to get to the basement. I could've sworn someone was in the kitchen, I just felt something. I called "Hello?" again, but no answer. I reached the door and looked down into the basement, and at the bottom of the stairs there was my girlfriend. She was buried in the dirt floor up to her shoulders, her head tilted to one side.

I thought I screamed, but I don't remember any sound coming out. I nearly fell down the stairs to get to her, and when I saw she was catatonic my heart stopped beating for a second.

I began to dig through the dirt floor. Over and over I said her name and tried to get her to wake up. I thought maybe if I started talking, just talking like we were hanging out together, it might get her to come around. I'd heard somewhere that sometimes worked with comatose patients.

We were going to watch the movie *Blood Simple* the other night, but never got around to it. Connie had never seen it before. It was one of the movies on our list of thrillers we'd been working through. Last week we watched *Shallow Grave*.

"The best part about *Blood Simple* is the ending, so we'll have to watch it at some point. I won't give it away, but you'll like it. I know you didn't seem that into watching it, but trust me it's worth it for the cool ending. I don't want to give too much away, but Frances McDormand kicks ass as Abby!"

I suddenly got the strangest thought, that maybe if I told Connie the ending to it, she would snap out of it. She hated it when I spoiled endings for her, in books and movies. Sometimes, I just couldn't help it. I'd wait for her to read the book, but I'd want to talk about it so I'd reveal some things that happened. She called me the Spoiler Princess.

"I know you're going to kill me, but I just have to tell you the ending. So Ray is hiding out in the new apartment, and that creepy private detective guy is across the street with his gun aimed at the place. Abby comes in and turns on the light, and Ray tells her to turn it off because he's afraid they're being watched. Now remember, Abby doesn't think that her husband is dead. She thinks he's coming after them, Ray knows it's not him but he knows someone is after them. We know it's the private detective guy, but they don't.

"Abby flips the light back on, Ray takes a step forward and while they're talking a shot comes from across the street, hits Ray and he's dead! Abby ducks when another bullet comes through and crawls over to a spot underneath the window where she can't be seen from outside. Then she throws her shoes at the light bulb to smash it, so it's dark and he can't see in."

I stopped to take a breath, and checked to see what Connie was doing. Nothing had changed. She was still breathing, eyes open but not looking at anything. I didn't know what else to do but keep on digging and talking to her.

"So then the private detective guy starts to…"

Noises came from upstairs, like someone walking on the floor. I stopped and checked to see how far I'd gotten Connie out. I still had a long way to go. Why was it taking so long to dig her out? Then I realized, I was just digging through the dirt, not shoveling it. I wasn't putting it anywhere, so it was piling back onto itself like snow.

I wanted to cry my eyes out, then the basement door at the top of the stairs slammed shut. I panicked and backed away from Connie. There was an old washing machine

Dug Out

turned upside down in the corner and I crouched behind it. More noises from above. Then the door opened. I peeked around the washing machine and saw Connie's dad.

He walked down the stairs, slowly. The stairs creaked on every step as he walked. He's a big guy, so they would.

"Helloooo?" He called out in a singsong voice. "Is someone down here?"

I took a glance at Connie. It was obvious someone tried to dig her out. But I didn't come out from my hiding spot. Just because he knew I was down there, it didn't mean I had to give in that easily.

"You're going to enjoy the show, wherever you are!" He laughed and clapped his hands together. Then he pulled a metal folding chair out from behind the staircase. He opened it, and it creaked. It creaked again when he sat down on it, facing Connie. That's when I saw he had something in his hand, some long metal wire with a bright green square attached to it. It was a fly swatter, and he slapped Connie across both cheeks with it.

"Well little girl, you've gotten yourself into a real mess now haven't you?"

The realization of how insane her dad was had been sinking in since I'd found Connie buried in the dirt. I always knew this fucker was nutty. But I never realized just how insane he was until he said Connie got herself into this situation. According to him, she's at fault for being buried up to her neck like that. He's like one of those guys who would hit a woman and say "Look what you made me do!" That's pretty much the definition of delusional.

I felt the tears coming. They washed away the dirt that was on my face. My fear turned into anger as I watched him slap Connie with the fly-swatter. It was somehow worse than hitting her with his hands. I wanted to hit him with something of my own, and I looked around the washing machine but didn't see anything I could use.

Connie's dad stopped slapping her and stood up. I held my breath and watched him. He placed the fly-swatter on the chair and shuffled over to the shelves that held a bunch of preserves and canned soup, and disappeared around the corner. Then I heard the door that leads to the backyard open and he left, shutting the door behind him.

I came out from behind the washing machine, but just stood there because I didn't know exactly what to do. Do I keep digging out Connie? Do I look for some kind of weapon? Do I run upstairs and call for help? Or do I peek outside to see what Connie's dad is doing, and that's what I went to do. But then I heard the door open and I rushed back to my hiding place.

I waited for the sound of the door closing, but it didn't happen. I heard Connie's dad mumbling and some clinking noises, like he was moving glass jars around. Then he grunted and the door closed, but he didn't walk into the basement. I peered around the side of the washing machine, but he wasn't there. He must've just grabbed something and then went right back out.

So I waited a minute, then crept out again. I tiptoed over to the tiny basement window, but it was starting to get dark and I couldn't really see anything. I was worried her dad would see me, so I did one of the other things on my to-do list and looked for a weapon of some sort. My first impulse was to look around the shelves near the door, but I was afraid to be too close to the door in case he came right back. What the hell was he doing anyway?

So I went to the other side of the basement, hoping to find something in the storage area. There wasn't much besides a bunch of stuff from Connie's childhood. An old rocking horse and a tricycle, some clear plastic bins with dolls and jump ropes, her old pompoms and batons. Next to that was a bin marked "baby clothes" and another marked "dance clothes."

I went back to the bin with her old cheerleading stuff. Specifically the one with batons. I rushed over to it and snapped the top off, rifled through red and white pompoms and grabbed one of the batons. It was hard plastic with rubber ends, and I knew a baton wouldn't be much of a weapon but it was the best I could do. I hid behind the washing machine, and a few seconds later Connie's dad came back into the basement.

He went over to his chair and brought it closer to her. He had a knife and a piece of wood. He was carving the wood into something I couldn't make out. And he started whistling. Whistling, what a sicko! I looked at Connie, and could've sworn she twitched. That made me feel better, she was still with me.

"I haven't seen that little friend of yours," he said and cleared his throat. "But I suspect she's around."

He chuckled and looked toward my hiding spot. My palms were sweating so badly the baton slipped and almost hit the washing machine. I gasped, a bit too loudly. Connie's dad laughed and resumed whistling.

I tightened my grip on the baton, and it suddenly felt like an even lesser weapon compared to his knife and whatever he was fashioning that piece of wood into. Not to mention the fact that he was about five times my size.

At least I could try to stop him from hurting Connie. I just didn't know what he was planning to do. If he was carving the wood into a weapon, why didn't he just use the knife? And if he was going to kill us, why hadn't he done it already?

I focused on the piece of wood. It looked like he was carving it into the shape of a gun, and he appeared to be done with it. He put down the knife and blew excess shavings off the wooden gun and held it up.

That's when I realized what it was. It wasn't a wooden gun, it was a wooden dick. Though the difference between the two in reality is slight. They're both so similar in shape, and action. Menacing and dangerous, piercing you with a bullet that can do lots of damage. No wonder I've never been attracted to guys.

"You see what this is sweetheart?" He smiled and pointed it at Connie. "I've been working on this ever since you told me you think you're a man. This is what makes you a man, so…I made one for you!" He shook with laughter and I shook my head in disgust.

"But we'll save that for later."

He put it down on the floor next to the knife. That knife was a far better weapon than the stupid baton I was holding, but it was too far away, and too close to him.

"For now, I've got a real one for you!"

Connie's dad unzipped his pants and pulled out his own dick. It looked disgusting, filthy and hairy. I felt nauseous again, and kept my mouth closed tight.

He crouched down next to Connie holding it in his hands, and hit her across the face with it. This was even worse than the fly-swatter. Then he opened up her mouth. Now I really felt like I was going to throw up.

"I'll teach you to like it sweetheart. It's natural, it's what God intended…"

Really, and God also intended for a father to abuse his daughter like this? Connie was so out of it, I hoped she had no idea what was going on. He started to inch toward her mouth, and I realized he was farther from the knife. I knew it was my chance, so I crept out from behind the washing machine. I ran over to the knife and grabbed it. He didn't even see me until I had the knife pointed at him.

"Stop it you fucking asshole!"

"And what do you think you're going to do with that, little girl?"

He pulled away from Connie and laughed, but I could tell he was nervous since he tucked it back into his pants. That gave me a feeling of power and I took a step closer and pointed the knife at him.

"You're going to dig out Connie, and then we're leaving. You'll never see either of us again, I promise you that."

"I can't let my daughter leave. She's my responsibility."

"She's eighteen, she's an adult. You can't tell her what to do."

"Neither can you, my little dyke!"

He reached out and tried to grab the knife. I backed up and swiped at him with it. It missed his arm by inches. He grabbed for it again, and this time when I backed up I hit the chair and stumbled. He grabbed my arm that held the knife, and twisted it so hard I felt like it was going to snap. Tears welled up in my eyes, but I wouldn't give him the satisfaction of hearing me cry.

"Let go or I'll break that arm of yours!" He twisted harder. I dropped the knife.

He slapped me across the face and picked up the knife. I wanted to kill him so badly at that moment as this rage bubbled up inside of me. Years of playing various sports made the muscles in my young legs so strong and supple, I wished that same strength had been in my arms. I could've fought him harder when he went for the knife. Women are stuck with strength in our legs, not in our arms, but it comes in handy when you have to kick a man in the balls. Which is exactly what I did.

I summoned up all of that rage and energized it into the massive kick I laid into his groin, and I actually felt him stumble back from the force of it. He screamed and dropped the knife with his hand on his crotch. I grabbed the knife and stood up, and that's when I saw Connie's mom.

She was standing at the top of the stairs holding a gun, for how long I had no idea. She could've been watching the whole scene between me and her husband.

"Stop it right there," she said and pointed the gun at me.

It had a silencer attached to it, like I'd seen in movies. I lowered the knife but didn't drop it. Connie's dad was whimpering, and I heard a soft cough that I hoped was Connie's. I looked back at her mom.

Connie's mom had always been very timid, never questioning her husband and dutifully tending to chores and meals. Connie always said, "I hope that crap isn't hereditary!"

Seeing her mom holding a gun with a calm look on her face was a shock. I had been basking in my triumph over kicking Connie's dad, and now her mom was apparently just as crazy. We were screwed. I was never getting Connie out, and they were going to kill me.

"This is what's going to happen." Connie's mom took a few steps down the stairs.

"You're going to take Connie and get away from here. I'll help you dig her out. But first I'm going to shoot my husband."

She turned, pointed the gun and shot Connie's dad. I saw the bewildered look on his face as the bullet went through the center of his forehead.

I gasped and sucked in air since it felt like the wind had been knocked out of me. Connie's mom stepped around me and took down a plastic shovel that was hanging on the wall. How I'd missed that when I first got into this I have no idea. Guess I was too focused on Connie. Her mom started to shovel the dirt away.

"Can I get some help? There's another shovel over there."

Wow. There were two shovels I'd missed. I ran to grab the shovel. We not only had to get her out of there but get her to a hospital.

"I don't know what else to say but thank you!" I began to dig.

"You might not want to do that just yet. I'm going to tell the police that you and Connie killed my husband."

I stopped and stared at her.

"Don't worry, I'm going to tell them it was self-defense, and that I don't want to press charges. I just needed a patsy."

Connie's mom, who had never said anything else to me besides "Want some lemonade?" or "Are you staying for dinner?" was talking like some character in a thriller. Who was she, exactly?

"This horrible man was abusing me in every sense of the word, but I wasn't going to jail for killing him. Perhaps I could've left him, but I didn't want to leave Connie alone with him. I also didn't want to lose the home I've built over the years. But as soon as Connie told us her big news last week, I started thinking about how I could use you as my patsy."

"So what are you going to tell the cops?"

"Exactly what happened, but I'll say that you found the gun and used it on him after he tried to stab you with the knife. I'll tell them all about his homophobia, but not about the abuse toward me since that will make me a suspect, and I'll play the grieving widow very well. Sorry to put it on you two, but you won't be around this town to worry about it anyway."

We finished digging Connie out, then took her to the hospital where they hooked up IVs and gave her fluids, and overnight she suddenly woke up. She didn't remember anything about what happened, and for that I'm grateful.

After the cops questioned me, and made sure my story corroborated with what Connie's mom told them, we moved to our little place in Boston. Connie's temping and I got a job at the Museum of Fine Arts. Her mom comes to visit sometimes, and we've made a bunch of new friends and have set up a nice little life for ourselves.

Though sometimes when I go down on Connie, when I put my tongue really deep inside of her, I can somewhat taste dirt. It's diluted and faint, very faint, but I swear it's there. She tells me it's all in my head, and we laugh about it. Connie says it gives brand new meaning to "nappy dugout." I love her for saying stuff like that.

Casualties of Encounters

Susie Dietz leaned toward the window and lifted up a slat of the Venetian blinds. She looked out at the hotel parking lot. When her phone rang and she saw Avery Wynn's number flash on the display, she rolled her eyes and picked it up. She kept the phone close to her ear while listening to Avery's stammering on the other end. When he stopped to take a breath, she spoke.

"Avery, you're the one who cheated on Meredith. How is that my fault?"

"You said total discretion! Why the hell did you send her that video of us in bed together?"

"I just couldn't live with myself anymore. The guilt was tearing me up inside."

Susie made her voice crack to sound like tears were coming. She stepped back from the window and twirled a lock of her auburn hair between her thumb and forefinger.

"Guilt? You manipulating little slut! I'll kill you for this!"

With a beep, Avery was gone. Susie stared at the phone in her hand and after several seconds she put it down and chewed on her thumbnail.

She reassured herself that Avery wouldn't do anything, that he was just blowing off steam. She peered through the blinds again. No movement in the parking lot.

She sat down at the writing table and gazed around the hotel room, what must be the hundredth one she'd stayed in since her divorce. Across from her was the bureau, and she caught her reflection in the mirror above it.

"How did I get here?" Susie asked her reflection as she thought back to her teenage years.

Her mother had believed in saving yourself for marriage, and Susie followed her advice. She only allowed an evening to end in oral sex, and remained a technical virgin until she was married.

She met her future husband Jason Dane at college in Rhode Island. They were both members of the Student Activities Council, and always ended up on the same side in debates over function themes and events. His eyes were the same color green as hers, too. They began dating, and Susie ignored the rumors that Jason was sleeping with other women on the side. She told herself the other girls were just jealous since he was one of the most sought-after boys at school.

Jason proposed to her their senior year, and six months after graduation they were married. Susie had been dreaming about their wedding night for so long, she was expecting it to be the most magical night of her life. She was incredibly disappointed when Jason groaned in less than a minute upon entering her, rolled over and fell asleep. She told herself it was the champagne, and that it would be better next time.

Several months into the marriage, when Jason's prowess hadn't changed, she reassured herself that there were more important things in a marriage than sex. She focused on being a dutiful housewife and hoped she would get pregnant soon so she could focus on being a good mother.

One day after she'd finished folding the laundry, a rolled up pair of socks dropped from the basket and fell under the bed. Susie crouched down and lifted the bed skirt, and something shiny caught her eye.

It was some sort of foil wrapper, and for a moment she wondered if Jason had a secret habit of eating candy in bed. When she picked it up and saw what it was, she realized he did indeed have a secret habit in their bed. It was part of a condom wrapper made of silvery orange foil, with tiny words boasting "tropical flavor."

She flung it to the floor and shuddered all over. She fell to her knees as her eyes filled up with tears. After crying for several minutes, she picked up the wrapper and walked into the bathroom. She wrapped it up in toilet paper and threw it into the trash, which she promptly brought outside to the barrels. She never mentioned finding the condom wrapper. She told herself it must have gotten caught on the bottom of her shoe somehow, and put it in the back of her mind.

Several months later she was sorting laundry while Jason was at work. She emptied the pockets of his slacks before tossing them into the machine and found a piece of paper. Written on it was a telephone number above the name Mitzi.

Susie sighed and cried softly for a few minutes as she looked at it. Then she tore up the paper and threw it away. She never mentioned it to Jason, and tried to forget about it. But then the neighbors brought home a Labrador they named Mitzi. Every time they called the dog she cringed.

Three years later, Jason announced that he was leaving her for another woman. A barista named Becky. Susie didn't enjoy recalling her reaction at the time, which consisted of throwing herself to her knees and begging Jason to stay. But she found it therapeutic to relive that moment as a way to fuel her motivation for her current work.

Jason granted her a generous alimony and left her the house, but she put the house on the market and moved into a hotel room. She found the leisure and anonymity of hotel life quite comforting. The concierge only bothered her with offerings from the spa, and whether or not she'd like a wake-up call. Her bed was made every day without her lifting a finger, and she toned her body with daily laps in the pool followed by massages.

One evening she was enjoying a glass of chardonnay at the hotel bar, and noticed she'd caught the attention of a man perched on a stool at the corner end. He was stout with greasy hair, and wasn't very attractive to Susie. He raised his glass toward her, and she returned the gesture with a polite smile. He took it as a sign of encouragement, sauntered over and sat down next to her.

"Evening," he said. "Buy you a drink?"

"Well, I'm not quite finished with this one." Susie held up her wineglass.

"After that?"

"We'll see."

He talked about his construction business that was developing an upcoming condominium. Susie nodded and sipped her drink. She responded vaguely to his questions, which included her dating situation and what brought her to the hotel.

"You here all by yourself?"

"Yes."

"Want some company tonight?"

The man turned his head and looked directly into Susie's eyes. He cocked an eyebrow, and in that instant, he slightly resembled Jack Nicholson.

Many things about this man did not appeal to her, but his audaciousness and his Jack Nicholson eyebrows sent tingles down her spine. Perhaps she simply wanted to be close to someone again, though she didn't give it much thought at the time. Soon she was naked underneath him. When he entered her she had the most amazing rush of adrenaline course through her body. This man was nothing like Jason, the only one she'd ever been with. She wrapped her legs around his waist and thrust with him.

Jason had always finished so early, but this man didn't stop until Susie moaned when she felt waves breaking throughout her body. It was the most incredible feeling she'd ever had. She never asked for the man's name, and never revealed hers. He left her room two hours before sunrise, and she never saw him again.

Susie experienced her first orgasm that night, and she was left desperately wanting another. She went to the hotel bar again that evening, met a new man and had him to her room. She never asked for his name, either.

The anonymous sex with a stranger, like the anonymous hotel room, became an addiction for her.

She spent the next year of her life living in hotels, never staying in one room for longer than a few weeks. After a while, she began getting snide looks from some of the hotel employees, since she was bringing so many different men to her room. In one hotel, the manager accused her of solicitation and threatened to call the police. Susie checked out immediately, and reserved a room at a new hotel twenty miles away.

In each hotel she had a new encounter with a strange man. Sometimes they exchanged names and sometimes they met again, and when she grew bored with meeting men in bars she decided to peruse the dating personals. She wasn't looking for anything serious and avoided sites like Match and eHarmony. She liked the anonymity of Craigslist with its Casual Encounters section.

Susie read through the ads, got an idea of what she wanted to say, and wrote her first post:

Newly divorced, 29, attractive, slim, green eyes. Interested in meeting men aged 25-45 for casual encounters. Please include a picture. Looks aren't important, but attraction is.

Her inbox swarmed with responses, but then she saw that many were advertisements for help with dysfunctional erections, and many others were from men who did nothing but provide close-up pictures of their erections.

After she weeded through the emails and put together a small group of men, she picked one and set up her first meeting. His name was Andy Burns, and she discovered the drawback to meeting men online was the likelihood of it becoming too personal. They chatted before meeting and he revealed tidbits about his life. He had a trust fund and a country club membership, and liked to play squash.

She met him at her hotel for a drink, and though the sex was enjoyable she didn't plan on ever meeting him again. She found the sex much more exciting when she knew as little about the men as possible.

As Andy pulled on his boxers, his phone on the bedside table beeped.

"Do you need to get that?"

"Nah, probably just my wife, checking up on me."

Susie's mind reeled as she stared at the phone.

"You're…you're married?"

"Oh yeah, I thought I mentioned that. It's no big deal, I've been doing this for years. She has no idea, don't worry!"

Andy picked up his phone and looked through his call list. He winked at her and tossed his phone onto the bed, and went into the bathroom. Susie's eyes narrowed as she looked at the phone. He'd never mentioned he was married. If he had, she never would have agreed to meet him. She wondered how many of the other men she'd encountered were married, and shuddered at the thought.

She felt pity for Andy's wife, whose name she felt the need to know. While he was in the bathroom, she picked up his phone. It hadn't locked yet, so she could see that he had two missed calls from Helen Burns. She grabbed a pen and pad from the drawer and scribbled down Helen's number. Susie heard the toilet flush, and she put the phone back and moved to the other side of the room. She folded the piece of paper with Helen's number and placed it in the pocket of her robe.

The next day Susie ordered room service and nibbled on a club sandwich while she stared at Helen's number and grappled over what to do with it.

She sometimes wished she had done things differently with Jason. Confronted him the moment she found the condom wrapper. Maybe if she had, he would have felt guilty enough to stop his affairs and work on their marriage.

Susie sighed and picked up the paper with Helen's number. She called her and left a message, stating she was a friend of her husband's. Ten minutes later Helen returned the call.

"Hello, this is Helen Burns. You left me a message?"

"Yes, hello. My name is Susie, and I'm calling about your husband Andy."

"Is he all right?"

"Yes, though it depends on what you mean by 'all right.' Listen Helen, there's something you should know…"

Susie paused a beat.

"He's cheating on you."

Susie listened carefully. She heard jagged breathing on the other end of the phone, and suspected Helen was going through a shock similar to the one she'd had years ago after discovering her husband was unfaithful.

"How did you get my number?" Helen finally spoke, and her tone had changed. It was sharp and all business.

"Well, I...to be honest, I slept with him, but I had absolutely no idea he was married, seriously! As soon as I found out, I went into his phone and got your number. I know we don't know each other, but I felt you needed to know."

"I see."

"Thing is, I was married and my husband cheated on me. I never confronted him and it blew up in my face. I thought it was my duty to let you know, so hopefully the same thing doesn't happen to you."

"Well thank you for informing me, Miss..."

"Dane...I mean, Dietz. Susie Dietz."

"Miss Dietz. Thank you for the information. Good day."

Helen ended the call. Susie felt elated, and wished she could witness Andy's reaction once his wife confronted him. She felt she'd done a good deed, the kind that doesn't happen every day. She thought if that could be a job, she'd be great at it. She'd make a career out of exposing cheating husbands to their wives. She laughed at that thought while taking a shower. Later while she dried her hair, she started seriously thinking that she should in fact make a career out of it.

It had been so easy to lure men to her hotel room for casual sex. She thought about how easy it would be to secretly record the sex with a hidden camcorder like a nanny cam, then burn a DVD on her laptop. That way she wouldn't even have to talk to the wives, just send them a disc that would speak for itself. The hard part would be finding out their addresses.

That evening she visited the Casual Encounters section and searched through the ads of men looking for women. She was surprised at how brazen the men were. They had no shame in blatantly stating in their posts that they were married, but seeking discreet fun.

Susie was snapped out of her flashback by her phone vibrating. She looked at her phone and the name Meredith Wynn came on the screen. Susie chewed on her thumbnail and picked up the call.

"Hello?"

"Is this Susie Dietz?"

"Yes."

"It's Meredith, Avery's wife. You remember Avery, your newest victim?"

"I don't refer to them as the 'victims.' We, the women, are the victims here."

"My dear, you knowingly slept with a married man. And from what I understand, it's been several married men over quite some time. You are hardly a victim."

"Listen Meredith, the only reason I revealed to you what I do is that I thought you were smart and could handle it. I actually thought you'd be impressed with my work."

"Work? This is considered work to you?" Meredith let out a dry chuckle.

"Yes." Susie sighed. "It is, as a matter of fact. Anyway, is there a reason you called?"

"It may please you to know that I'm leaving Avery. He and I are separated, and will soon be divorced."

"That's wonderful."

"Is it? Is it really wonderful, being the catalyst to a broken marriage? True, Avery and I had our problems. I suspected his philandering on more than one occasion, but it's not like I didn't indulge in the pleasure myself from time to time."

"What?"

"Avery and I had an unspoken open marriage. He never asked me, I never asked him, and we were getting along just fine. But then he slept with you. I was forced to leave him when my sister-in-law saw that lovely film you sent. I couldn't very well stay married to him with that embarrassment hanging over me."

Susie was silent.

"Be careful, my dear. Be very careful. One of these days you might meddle in the wrong marriage. Take care now."

Meredith hung up on her end. Susie held the phone and stared at it for a few seconds. She put it down and walked over to the closet, pulled out her suitcase and opened it. Inside was a three-ring binder. She opened the cover and flipped through her scrapbook, and reminisced about each encounter as she turned the pages.

There was a picture of Andy Burns with printouts of their email exchanges. She turned the pages until she reached a picture of a balding man with dark eyes, and the name Mitch Kitteridge printed underneath.

Mitch was Susie's second married man, and the first one she targeted. After the Andy situation, she began a hunt online for married men for the sole purpose of revealing them to their wives, and it had turned into an obsession. One that she didn't really want to end.

Casualties of Encounters

Mitch's ad said he was looking for an attractive woman with an open mind. When Susie discovered he was into spanking and bondage she saw just how important the open mind part was. Before their meeting, she did some tests with the hidden camcorder to make sure it was angled properly, and set it up to record just before he arrived.

After their romp with fuzzy handcuffs and a tickle whip, Susie watched the video and burned a copy on her laptop. She was impressed with how good she looked in the video. All of her massages and laps in the pool had paid off.

She found Mitch's home address easily enough by googling his phone number. She sent the disc to his wife Adele, with a short note that said: "A hobby of your husband's you might find interesting," and signed it "a friend."

Not long after that, Mitch called her and told her that Adele had left him. He didn't seem angry about the video, he was actually turned on by it, and asked her if she'd be interested in dating now that he was single. Susie declined, then switched hotels.

She moved on to her next married man, Bob Capreze, whose photo she flipped to in the scrapbook. He was a handsome lawyer with a private practice and a debutante wife named Lisa. What Susie hadn't been prepared for was Lisa Capreze's reaction. After she watched the video, she stabbed Bob in the stomach and attempted to run down Susie in the parking lot of the hotel.

Susie shuddered when she recalled the silver Mercedes-Benz that nearly hit her, and she landed into a bush on her backside. A beautiful blond woman screeched at Susie to stay away from her husband, and then sped away with tires squealing against the pavement. The next day Susie read in the paper about the prominent lawyer Robert J. Capreze who had been stabbed but was expected to make a full recovery.

Susie exhaled as she flipped past Bob's entry in her scrapbook. That had scared her off for a while. It wasn't until she got her final divorce papers from Jason that she felt the urge to find another married man. She promised herself she would move to a different hotel before mailing the disc to the wife.

Her next encounter was Sammy Kowalski. He was a car salesman who incessantly complained about his wife Beth, a plump redhead with a penchant for online shopping and cookie dough ice cream. According to Sammy, he and Beth had had sex only a dozen times in their five-year marriage.

Susie imagined how much cookie dough Beth would eat when she saw Sammy having wild sex with another woman while he said things like "Beth would never let me do that!"

After she sent the video, she didn't hear anything from Sammy or his wife which was strange, and it worried her. But then one day she was walking through the mall and saw Sammy holding hands with a redheaded woman whom Susie assumed was Beth. When they spotted her, Beth screamed and Sammy put his arm around her, and yelled at Susie to stay away from them. Susie ran out of the mall and went back to her hotel. At first she was surprised that Beth had forgiven Sammy, but then remembered that she had begged her husband to stay after his infidelity.

She turned the page and saw the photograph of Ryan MacLeod, a rugged minor league baseball player. He and his wife Josie were married right after high school, and Josie had been saving herself for marriage. Much to Ryan's chagrin her inexperience made her so timid it affected their sex life, so he began to look outside of their marriage for assertive, older women. His ad caught Susie's attention because he made a reference to being in love with his wife and had no intention of ending his marriage.

Susie felt a kinship with Josie since they'd both saved themselves for marriage only to have their husbands cheat on them. She had mixed feelings after sending Josie the disc. On the one hand she felt the pain Josie was about to go through, but was also happy that she was still young enough to start her life over.

The next page in the scrapbook was blank. She hadn't yet added the latest entry, Avery Wynn. She chuckled as she thought back to his empty threats over the phone that morning, but then she thought about the call from Meredith, and her warning.

She flipped through the rest of the scrapbook, and the dozens of empty pages waiting to be filled. She felt there was still so much work to do. There were so many cheating husbands out there, as the personal ads showed.

The house she'd shared with Jason had been sold for some time, but Susie hadn't yet put a down payment on a new home. She had to admit that hotel life wasn't as glamorous as it used to be, and the thought of finding a new house or a condo and settling somewhere was appealing. She had her Bachelor's in History, and wasn't doing anything with it. Before she met Jason, she'd been planning on attending law school after college. She thought it was maybe time to reconsider that.

Susie decided to visit the hotel spa, get a massage and think things over. She wasn't sure if she was ready to take on a new challenge. She was still getting used to being single and discovering her sexuality. Even though hotel life was losing its appeal, it was still comforting in its consistency.

The masseuse she had that day was a middle-aged woman who liked to talk. Susie didn't mind, and gave her the polite murmurs throughout the hour. But when the masseuse complained about her brother-in-law cheating on her sister, Susie felt a tingle down her spine that told her she definitely wasn't done with her work yet.

That night, she went online and searched for her next married man. The ad that caught her eye was from a man looking for a long-term affair, and emphasized his need for discretion. She responded to the ad and attached a picture of herself. Several minutes later she received a response from George Huntington with a photo of a dark-haired man wearing an Italian suit. She invited him for a drink at her hotel.

George was an investment banker who played golf and had a wife named Annabelle. Susie pretended she was still married to Jason, and talked about his affairs with other women as her reason for looking elsewhere.

She invited him up to her room, the camcorder already set up. He took off his clothes, walked over to Susie and undressed her. She found George to be an extremely gentle lover. He went down on her for a long time, and he didn't want to spank her, or tie her up, or have anal sex. Quite a difference from the other husbands she'd been with.

George even wanted to cuddle afterward, but Susie declined saying she had to meet her husband. She promised George they would meet again soon, and collected his home address from an electric bill inside his briefcase while he showered.

After he left, Susie took a shower and felt torn over what to do. She dried off and sat at her laptop, opened the email from George and stared at his picture. He looked like a sleazy businessman, but in reality he was nothing like that.

She looked at his wife's name scrawled next to their address. She took the flash drive out of the camcorder and put it on top of the notepad.

"If you don't send a disc, what was the point of all that?" Susie asked herself.

She shook her head and placed the flash drive with the notepad inside the dresser drawer. She ordered room service and watched television before going to bed that night.

When she woke up the next morning, she immediately copied the video of her and George to her laptop and burned it to DVD before she could change her mind. Later on that day she mailed the disc to Annabelle, and decided that she would take a break from her work for a while. That night she went online, but instead of searching for married men she researched law schools.

Over the next few days, Susie was so wrapped up in her new plan to go to law school that she didn't bother to change hotels. She ignored the calls from George, which stopped after a couple of days. One night after she treated herself to a cheeseburger and fries, Susie logged into her email and discovered a message from George. An angry email was to be expected, especially after the ignored phone calls.

The message subject was "Susie," and at first she thought the email was blank but she scrolled down and saw something small on the screen. There was only one word in the middle of the page:

dies

For a split second she thought it was her surname. When she registered what word it was, she felt a chill. Susie deleted the message and went back to her inbox. Several seconds later three more messages from George Huntington appeared, one after the other, all entitled "Susie."

With trembling hands she opened the first one, and again thought it was a blank message. She scrolled with her forefinger, her shoulders hunched over the laptop. She chewed on her thumbnail, her eyebrows furrowed as she read the new message, which also contained one word in small font:

tonight

She wanted to slam the laptop shut and run out of the hotel, but she wanted to see what the other messages said first. She closed that email and opened the next one, which held a smaller word she nearly missed:

for

Susie opened the last message with wide eyes and read the lone word that was in all caps:

ANNABELLE

Susie sucked in her breath and ran over to the door. She slammed the latch shut and checked the deadbolt. She stood on her toes and peered through the peephole, but all she could see was the door to the room across from her.

She looked down and saw a tray with a half-eaten sandwich and empty ketchup packets. Susie exhaled and went back to the laptop, where her inbox showed a new message from George. This one was entitled "Annabelle," and had an attachment.

The message itself was blank, Susie checked three times. She opened the attachment, and it displayed a picture of a woman she assumed was Annabelle. She had strawberry blond hair, a slim figure and long legs. She was also naked, lying in a bathtub filled with dark pink water. Her right arm was split open from elbow to wrist. Her left arm had a much smaller cut. In the soap dish was a bloody razor. Her eyes were closed and the bloodied water reached up to her chin.

Just then Susie's phone vibrated, and she jumped up so quickly the laptop toppled over and fell to the carpet with a soft thud. She picked up her phone and saw George's number on the screen. Her hands shook as she held the phone to her ear.

"She's dead, you fucking bitch. You killed her with that video of us! I told you I needed to be discreet! She was on edge, she couldn't handle this. What the fuck have you done?"

"She..." Susie stammered. "She...she k-killed herself?" Her voice cracked toward the end, and she placed a hand over her mouth. She dropped the phone as tears streamed down her cheeks. She didn't hear George's next words because her ears were ringing.

"Didn't you get my message? You're next."

George was gone from the other end with a beep. Susie fell to the floor and rocked back and forth as she wept. Her laptop lay on its side with the picture of Annabelle in the tub at a horizontal angle. Susie's vision was impaired from the tears in her eyes, and it wasn't until she retrieved a tissue from the nightstand that she noticed the picture of Annabelle, screamed and kicked the laptop shut. She felt an unpleasant belch rising and ran into the bathroom where she vomited in the toilet.

While she rinsed out her mouth in the sink, foot shadows appeared through the bottom slat of the door to the room. A pounding knock made Susie jump, and she pulled a metal nail file out of her make-up bag and tiptoed to the door. The loud knock came again. She looked through the peephole, sure that George was standing there with a crazed look in his eyes.

It was one of the hotel desk clerks. His maroon vest and matching tie brought a rush of comfort. She unlatched and opened the door, with furtive glances down the corridor.

"Good evening, Ms. Dietz. We tried contacting you over the phone but there was no answer."

"Oh, I completely forgot about putting the 'Do Not Disturb' on my phone."

"No problem ma'am, just wanted to give you a message from a gentleman who was in earlier today looking for you."

"Oh?"

"Yes, it seemed quite urgent."

The clerk handed her a cream-colored envelope, with just her first name typed on it. The envelope was tightly sealed, and embossed with a gold letter "H" on the return address section.

"Thank you."

Susie took the envelope as the clerk turned and walked away. She closed the door and secured every lock, sat on the bed, and opened it.

Inside was a note card, the same color, and texture as the envelope. Two words, "dies tonight," were written in the middle.

Susie ran to the closet and grabbed her suitcase. She tore through the room throwing clothes into the suitcase without folding anything. She stuffed her make-up bag and threw it on top of the clothes. The laptop and camcorder went into her leather duffel bag that she slung over her shoulder, and she slammed her feet into a pair of mules that looked out of place with the sweatpants she wore.

After a final sweep through the room for her belongings, Susie forced her suitcase closed and pulled it behind her as she left. She hurried to the elevator, and heard footsteps approaching. She pushed the button over and over as the footsteps grew closer. The elevator finally arrived and she threw the bags followed by herself inside and pushed the "Door Close" button.

She heard a man's voice asking her to hold the elevator and caught a glimpse of a gray-haired man just before the doors closed. Susie sighed and hung her head as the elevator descended.

When she reached the lobby and main desk, the same clerk who'd delivered the note was standing behind it.

"Ah, Ms. Dietz. I hope it wasn't bad news?"

Susie paused for a moment before answering. She thought it would be a good idea to throw George off track in case he came looking for her.

"Actually, yes. It's…a family emergency and I have to fly to…Chicago. I'll need to check out right away."

"Of course. I am sorry to hear that. Would you like me to call the airlines to see what flights are available?"

"No need, I've already booked something, but thank you. Please, as quickly as you can."

She tapped her room card on the desk and the clerk took it. After she paid the bill, Susie pulled her suitcase behind her and rushed outside. She watched for any signs of movement until she reached her Audi, and seconds later sped out of the hotel lot.

Susie had no idea where she was going, and figured she'd find a room at the next hotel she came across. She drove down the street and kept an eye out for hotel signs. She reached an entrance to the freeway, and on an impulse she turned onto it and merged with the light late-night traffic. To the left and right of her were dense woods with the occasional sign warning of deer crossing. Susie wiped tears from her eyes and concentrated on the road, and tried not to think about Annabelle lying in a bathtub with blood coming out of her wrists.

"Hello Susie." The voice of George Huntington came from the backseat. Then his face was in her rearview mirror. Susie screamed, slammed on the brakes and pulled the wheel to the right. The car skidded into the breakdown lane and scraped against the guardrail. George's hand covered Susie's mouth and his other hand grasped her throat. The car came to a halt as she pulled the emergency brake, and tried to release herself from George's grip.

"You killed her! You fucking killed her!" George said through clenched teeth. Susie managed to open her mouth enough to get a piece of his palm between her teeth, and bit down until she tasted blood.

George pulled his hand free. Susie opened the door and leaped out of the driver's side. She hit pavement with her knees and ignored the pain as she ran toward the road and waved her arms.

"Help me! He's trying to kill me!" She screamed, but none of the cars stopped. She reached into her pocket searching for her phone, but it wasn't there. She then remembered she'd placed it inside the cup holder in her car. Her car that George stepped out of gripping his bleeding hand.

Susie turned and climbed over the guardrail, kicked off her mules and dashed into the blackness of the woods. George followed, and she hid behind a thick tree. She tried to quiet her breathing since it was coming in short gasps. She shivered and heard twigs snapping.

"Susie! Where are you?" George's voice had turned into a growl.

She prayed he would walk right past her. When he did, she waited until his voice grew distant, and then inched her way back to the guardrail. Her socked feet made the sound of twigs snapping much quieter. When she got to the guardrail she climbed over and saw she wasn't very far from her car.

She ran over to it, but her cell phone wasn't in the cup holder. She rummaged around the floor and the backseat, but her phone wasn't anywhere in the car. She got into the driver's side and turned off the ignition, then re-started it. She put the car into gear, but it wouldn't move. It had jammed up against the guardrail so badly it was stuck to it. Susie hit the steering wheel with her palms and cried out as fresh tears came.

She looked up, and George stood on the other side of the windshield, grinning at her. He was holding her cell phone and waving it back and forth. Susie hauled herself out of the car, ran around the side and jumped back over the guardrail. George followed her into the trees again.

She ran deeper into the woods with George close behind. She glanced back to see how close, and tripped over a tree root and fell to the ground. In seconds, George was on top of her. He gripped her neck with both hands, and Susie's lungs gasped for air while her hands grasped the ground around her.

She grabbed something hard and sharp that felt like a rock, and hit George's head with it. He let go of her and toppled to the ground. She scrambled to her feet and ran, not bothering to look back.

Susie kept running, wondering how deep these woods really were, and finally had to stop to catch her breath. She backed up against a tree, her chest heaving. She knew someone would call the police about the car smashed against the guardrail, and when they found it empty they'd come into the woods searching. She figured all she had to do was wait and she'd be rescued eventually. She didn't check to see if George had been knocked out or not, but she didn't hear anything and thought she was safe for the time being.

As she took a step away from the tree, a hand shot out from around the other side and grabbed her wrist. Susie tried to yank free and George pulled her closer. With his other hand he gripped her neck, and then let go of her wrist to have both hands on her throat. He tightened his grip and Susie struggled against him. They twisted and turned together, and simultaneously slipped on a large tree root. Susie's foot twisted in the root, and she felt a painfully sharp snap in her ankle. She would've cried out if her air wasn't being cut off.

They landed on a large rock between two trees. There was a squishy, splintering noise as George's head bashed into a sharp, pointed edge that jutted out of the rock. Blood gushed out of George's temple, and his hands became slack on Susie's throat. She reached up and took his hands from her neck, and they fell limp against the rock.

Susie coughed and tried to sit up, but she felt dizzy and put her head back down. Her ankle throbbed, and when she tried to move sharp pain shot up through her calf and she shrieked.

She clamped a hand over her mouth and looked at George, expecting him to sit up and strangle her again, but he didn't move. She prodded him with a finger, and he twitched. Susie's heart jumped, but then he was still.

She looked down and her eyes adjusted to the dim moonlight that fell through the trees. She looked at his forehead and saw bits of gore that she guessed was brains, and bit her lip. He was definitely dead, and she would have felt relieved if her foot wasn't stuck in the tree root. She rummaged through George's pockets in the hopes that he still had her cell phone. He didn't, and didn't seem to have his own either.

A fresh wave of dizziness came over her. She fell back against the rock. She wanted nothing more than to simply fall asleep, and the rock was surprisingly comfortable.

She thought about her life before she met Jason, and how simple everything used to be. How desperately she wished to go back to that time. She thought about using her alimony money to start a fund in Annabelle's name, maybe something to do with suicide prevention. She wanted to go to law school. She wanted to stop sleeping with married men.

Jenna Moquin

Susie saw a bright light nearby. It was getting brighter, and she heard rustling noises and voices calling out. She closed her eyes and let the light shine over her. It made her feel comforted, like she was about to be saved.

The Donation

Marcus Adams set down his tumbler on the coaster, the glass shaking in his trembling, yellowed hand. His gaze caught the photo of him, James, Frederick and Rand, their arms around each other wearing their letterman sweaters. The left corner of his mouth went up in a half-smile as he focused on Rand's leering grin. The black and white photo didn't show the purple and gold of their school colors, or the flaming red color of Rand's hair. Marcus sighed as he tore his gaze away. Rand was the one he missed most of all.

It was nearing November and the weather at night was cold enough for a fire, but Marcus hadn't lit one. As soon as he'd arrived home he saw the envelope with the Stamden University logo in the mailbox, the purple and gold lettering that matched their letterman sweaters. His hands had begun trembling the moment he picked up the envelope, and they hadn't stopped shaking since.

When he read the letter that was inside his shoulders slumped. He sat in the chair next to the table and let the letter fall into his lap. For a few minutes, he sat there staring at the cabinet above the sink. Then he stood up, walked over to the sink and opened the cabinet.

Inside was a bottle of Dewar's scotch. He found it in the pantry at his last house when he'd cleaned it out one day after finding a mouse. He didn't remember buying it, though there were a lot of things he didn't remember buying back in his drinking days. But still he held onto the bottle, and brought it with him when he moved into this new dwelling.

Every once in a while he would gaze at the bottle to prove how strong he was. He could look at that bottle and not want a drink. The fact that it was Dewar's made it easier, since he'd never really cared for that brand. That little self-test had been going on for several months, and on the fourth of January he would've been sober for two years. He'd always known there was another reason he kept that bottle, though. It was his safety net.

The entire time he'd been attending AA meetings, he'd known deep down it was a sham. He said the prayer and listened to the stories from his fellow addicts, but he knew it was only a matter of time before he'd need that bottle. Just like he knew it was only a matter of time before one of those letters from Stamden arrived.

He opened the bottle and placed it under his nose. The smell was both comforting and nauseating at the same time. It certainly wasn't Lagavulin, but it would do. He poured some into a tumbler and spilled some onto the counter in the process.

Marcus went into the den and sat next to the fireplace. The room was cold, but the scotch kept him warm. He wanted a fire but didn't trust that his hands would cooperate with him. Perhaps he wouldn't bother getting a house with a fireplace for his next move, but he enjoyed sitting near a fireplace and reading. There was just something about it, even without a fire going.

He looked at the oak cane resting against the wall. So far he only needed it when the temperature dipped into the single digits, but his doctor told him it was only a matter of time until he'd need it year round.

The Donation

He gazed at the photo of him, Rand, Frederick and James in their crew sweaters. In the background of the photo he could see the edge of the quad. It had been a gorgeous autumn day. Marcus always found it odd that pictures taken at Stamden never came out clearly. The photographs always had a fuzziness to them.

He looked at the letter from Stamden. This time, they were inviting him to campus for a special Homecoming event on Thanksgiving weekend. He knew what they wanted, it was the same thing they always wanted, a donation.

Any college graduate knows you'll never go a year without a letter from your alma mater asking for money. It must work on some people, otherwise they wouldn't be so persistent about it.

What bothered him so much about this particular letter was the fact that he'd moved, and hadn't informed the school of his new address. He hadn't even informed the post office of his new address, and had so far only received mail addressed to the former residents.

What bothered him further was that the envelope had no postage on it. No date stamps from the post office, not even a prepaid meter label. It simply had his name and address written in calligraphy, Stamden University in the return address section, and a wax seal on the back. It had either appeared in his mailbox out of thin air, or someone had hand-delivered it.

Marcus didn't want to think about who might have crept up to his door and stuck the envelope inside. He settled the prickly feeling on the back of his neck by taking another drink. His gaze went back to the black and white photo, and he slipped into a memory.

* * * * *

It was a lovely October day in 1958, and Homecoming was just around the corner. Marcus and James walked out of Mumford Hall and stood with some of the other boys from Kappa Phi. They watched Rand do his impression of Jimmy Stewart for the girls from their sister sorority.

The girls from Phi Beta Gamma were sitting on the stone steps, their chiffon poodle skirts ruffling in the breeze. A few feet away Billy Darrell was tending to the hedges.

Billy Darrell's late father had been the school groundskeeper for over fifty years. One of the benefits of the job was that his children received free admission at Stamden for an undergraduate degree. His son Billy was a sophomore that year, and he had never quite fit in. Marcus had noticed he wasn't doing well in his classes either.

Billy was in basic Math and Science, what Marcus and Rand considered high school level, and yet he was still behind. He took courses like "rocks for jocks" that were put in place so star athletes and students of nepotism could coast by. But still Billy was struggling. He'd even failed an open book test.

As part of the scholarship, Billy was required to put in a certain amount of hours for the work study program. He alternated between assisting the new groundskeeper and working in the cafeteria.

Marcus thought working in the cafeteria was one of the worst jobs he could imagine. Scraping leftover sloppy joes from plastic trays and washing dishes with hardened gum stuck to the underside, not to mention cleaning up the messes from the weekly food fights.

He watched Billy trim the hedges with his clipper, then he flinched for whatever reason and nicked his finger on the blade. He was wearing gloves so wasn't really hurt, but instinctively put his finger up to his mouth and managed to get a leaf in there. He spit it out while coughing.

"Smooth move, Lawnmower!" Frederick called out, and laughed.

Billy stared at him. Frederick turned back toward the others, and Marcus watched as Billy raised his middle finger at Frederick.

"Holy smokes, he flipped you the bird!" Marcus laughed and tapped Frederick on the shoulder.

"He's got a lot of nerve." Rand nodded toward Billy.

Frederick looked back at Billy and mimicked his obscene gesture.

"Sit on it, Lawnmower!"

The bell rang for their next class, and Marcus trotted off with the rest of them. He stole a glance at Billy, still trimming the hedges and staring after them.

The photographer for the student newspaper was going around taking pictures for the Homecoming issue. He walked up to their group and asked for a photograph to represent the Kappa Phi fraternity.

"Of course!" Rand said with a grin. "Let's give something for the ladies!"

They all laughed and moved closer together, smiling at the bulb on top of the camera. Marcus was worried that he blinked right at the pop, but when he saw the photograph later he'd been happily surprised to see otherwise.

After the picture had been taken, Frederick told the photographer he would like to purchase framed copies so that all four of them could have it as a keepsake. Marcus had been impressed not just by Frederick's magnanimity, but how flush with cash he seemed to be. He realized that Frederick Boyd was a good friend to have in life.

* * * * *

Marcus was startled back to the present by creaking noises from above. It sounded like someone was walking on the floorboards upstairs.

His heartbeat quickened as he tried to get out of his seat, but he'd been sitting in the same position for so long his joints had grown stiff. He winced as he pulled himself out of the chair and took a few steps forward. He wasn't sure he wanted to investigate the noise. Part of him wanted to go back to his chair and feign sleep, pretend he didn't hear anything.

A gust of wind whipped through the windows. The floorboards above creaked again. He kept his eyes on the ceiling while he took another step forward. The wind outside picked up, and a soft howling blew throughout the house. Marcus shivered in his spot, and heard another creak. This one was directly above his head.

Suddenly there was rapping at his front door. Three quick knocks and then one more knock, softer than the others. Marcus turned in the direction of the foyer, and wondered who could be calling on him at this hour. Then he looked at his watch and saw it was just past six o'clock. He shook his head, went to the front door and chided himself for being such a child, frightened of noises.

He opened the door with the chain lock in place. No one was there. He grunted and unlatched the chain, then opened the door and poked his head outside.

The porch was empty, as was the path leading up to the house and the street beyond. The old porch swing that needed repairing creaked as it weaved back and forth. Marcus was startled for a moment and then realized the wind was just making the swing rock.

But what had caused the rapping at the door puzzled him. There were no tree branches nearby that could've banged against it in a heavy wind.

He sighed and went back inside. After he latched the chain on the door he went into the living room and peered through the window that overlooked the porch. He looked down the driveway and around the porch but saw nothing. He went back to the den and eyed the tumbler of scotch with a few sips left in it, and shook his head.

"That's what I get for falling off the wagon."

He remembered the stories he'd heard in AA from his fellow alcoholics. Many of them spoke of having hallucinations not only when they stopped drinking, but also when they went back to drinking after a long interval of sobriety.

Then he recalled the letter in his mailbox, and had a chill. He certainly hadn't hallucinated the letter. It was tangible. It even had a scent to it, a mixture of overcooked apple pie and that burnt leaf aroma of autumn bonfires. A scent that would bring a sense of nostalgia to an old alumnus, especially during Homecoming season. He deemed it a clever marketing ploy to lure a donation.

He picked up the glass and held it before him, figuring he might as well finish it off. Marcus raised the tumbler toward the photo of him with his friends.

He tilted his head back, brought the glass to his lips and downed the rest of the scotch. He went upstairs to bed and fell asleep, and dreamt about his days at Stamden. He slept so soundly he didn't hear the floorboards creak, even as they got closer to his bedroom.

* * * * *

English was Marcus' favorite subject, but it wasn't his major. His father didn't think there was much of a future with an English degree unless he was planning on going to law school, and he wasn't. He loved to read and write, and when he was younger had aspirations of becoming a bestselling novelist. He'd submitted a short story to a local magazine, but it had been rejected. He never submitted his writing anywhere else, it had stung that much.

He decided to settle upon the attitude of "if you can't be an athlete, be an athletic supporter" when it came to literature. He admired it and appreciated it, but didn't feel he had enough talent to compete with the rest of the writers out there, so he gave it up.

After his first couple Alcolics Anonymous meetings, he recalled it was soon after his decision to quit writing that he began drinking regularly. He would sneak into his father's liquor cabinet and take a nip of scotch here and there.

His father always received bottles of Lagavulin from his friends and colleagues for gifts. He was a difficult person to please, but there were two surefire things he loved, his Lagavulin and his Cuban cigars. The latter were difficult to obtain, so he mostly got the scotch for birthdays and Christmases. He had so many, he never noticed a pilfered bottle here and there.

That drink became Marcus's poison at the age of fifteen. He brought flasks to class with him, especially during final exams. He felt he tested better whilst inebriated. He hid the small flask in his sleeve and took a nip whenever he needed to, and his sleight of hand developed nicely with so much practice.

That little bit of secrecy that only he knew about gave him a feeling inside like he'd never had before. It was like being part of a secret society, even better than being in a fraternity. It was like a secret identity. He had something that no one else knew about, and it made him feel really good. Years later, after he joined AA, he realized in a depressing epiphany that his secret identity was being a lush.

One day in his Literature class, Marcus decided to take a quick drink while everyone was looking at James as he read from *Hamlet*. Professor Galen always chose James to read, something Marcus had noticed. He wasn't sure if she liked the way James read, or just liked James. He had always suspected there was something going on between James and their English professor.

Everyone watched as James read *Hamlet's* "To be or not to be" soliloquy. Marcus glanced around the classroom as he released the flask from his sleeve. He deftly uncapped it and brought it to his mouth, then folded his arms across his chest, re-capped the flask unseen and tucked it back into his sleeve. James stopped reading and Professor Galen clapped.

"Thank you, Mr. Melvin."

James sat down with a blush to his cheeks that didn't go unnoticed by Rand, who snickered and poked him in the ribs with his pencil.

"Jimbo's in love!"

"Don't call me Jimbo!" James whispered and looked up at Professor Galen.

After class, they went to the cafeteria for lunch. Marcus noticed Billy Darrell was mopping up an area of the linoleum near the back windows. He wondered if it had been another food fight or if someone had gotten sick. He eyed the goulash that was being served, and took his tray over to the sandwich bar.

He joined Rand and Frederick at a corner table that gave them full view of the cafeteria. Rand had his eye on the table two rows down from them where the cheerleaders were sitting. Marcus looked around to see what was holding up James, and didn't see him anywhere near the food lines.

"Where's James?"

"He said he forgot something back in English class," Rand said.

He glanced away from the cheerleaders long enough to wink at Marcus, and then brought his gaze back to their table. Frederick was fashioning a paper football and concentrating hard on it. When he was done he flicked it over to Billy Darrell, who was refilling the condiments near the sandwich bar. The paper football landed in the open jug of ketchup and some of it splashed up into Billy's face.

Billy stood frozen for a minute blinking ketchup out of his eyes. He looked toward their table where the Kappa Phi boys were smiling and laughing at him. He reached into the jug and pulled out the paper football, and threw it away. He began wiping the empty tables with a dishrag.

The boys moved over to the cheerleader's table and chatted with them about the upcoming race between Stamden and Harvard. All four of them were on the crew team. It was nearing the end of the lunch hour and most of the other students had cleared out. Frederick watched Billy as he got closer to their table, then purposefully knocked over a tray of half-eaten goulash.

The Donation

"You missed a spot, Lawnmower! Or should I say, Lunch Lady?"

Billy looked at the mess, and then at Frederick.

"Better go get your mop!" Frederick chuckled. Rand and Marcus giggled, and so did a couple of the cheerleaders. The rest of them had tight-lipped smiles on their faces.

"Too bad this school lets in lower life forms like this just because his daddy used to mow the lawn," Frederick said and tapped Rand on his shoulder. Rand shrugged and raised his eyebrows.

"Mowed the lawn, can you believe it?" Frederick continued. "My father donates thousands of dollars to this school every year. His father mowed the lawn, and he gets a free ride. Does that seem fair to you? Huh, Lawnmower?"

Billy threw down the wet rag in his hand, took several deep breaths and walked over to their table. He pointed at Frederick.

"His dangle is really small," Billy said. His voice was barely above a whisper and no one heard him.

"Did I give you permission to approach this table?" Frederick said with a smirk. Billy kept his finger pointed at him.

"Don't point your dirty finger at me!" Frederick snapped at him.

Billy's face grew red, and this time when he spoke the entire cafeteria heard it.

"You have the tiniest little dangle I ever saw!"

Several of the cheerleaders gasped. One of them had dated Frederick briefly. She laughed and then covered her mouth with her hand. Frederick stood up glaring at Billy.

"What was that, Lawnmower?"

"I saw it at the urinal," Billy said. "It's smaller than a pinky finger!"

Frederick grabbed Billy by his collar and slammed him against the concrete beam next to the table.

"You're a dead man, you filthy little…"

"Hey! Break it up over there!" The varsity coach walked into the cafeteria and rushed over to their table.

"Let go of him, Boyd!" The coach shouted at Frederick, who let go of Billy's shirt and backed off.

"Tyson and Adams," the coach said as he looked at Rand and Marcus. "Keep an eye on your friend here, make sure he doesn't do anything stupid!"

"Yes, sir," they said in unison.

"This ain't over, Lawnmower," Frederick whispered.

"Show's over folks, get back to class," the coach said.

They all cleared out of the cafeteria leaving Billy whimpering against the concrete beam.

* * * * *

Marcus woke up in a cold sweat. With a moan, he felt pressure in his bladder and pulled himself out of bed. His feet searched for his slippers that weren't at the bedside like they were supposed to be.

He stumbled toward the hallway and went to the bathroom and flicked on the light. He caught a glimpse of himself in the mirrored door of the medicine cabinet above the sink. His white frizzy hair framed the sides of his face. The bald spot on top of his head that had grown larger each year was almost to his ears now. His skin was yellowed from jaundice and his face held enough wrinkles to cover a lifetime. Shaking his head, he grunted at his reflection and

The Donation

wondered when this old man had come about. The changes aging brings happen so quickly sometimes.

He unbuttoned his pajama bottoms and relieved himself in the toilet. Being a man living alone, the seat was always up. He yawned and broke wind at the same time a floorboard creaked behind him, and he didn't hear it.

He flushed and yanked open the door to the medicine cabinet and looked at the row of prescription bottles on the bottom shelf. A mix of diuretics and beta-blockers, with some oxycodone and diazepam mixed in. Some had expired, some he hadn't used in a while, and some he wasn't supposed to use anymore but kept anyway in case he needed them.

He took out one of the diuretic tablets he was given for high blood pressure, and cursed himself for not taking it earlier. If he took it now he would definitely need to get up again soon to use the toilet. But he couldn't recall the last time he'd taken it and was worried about his blood pressure.

He swallowed the pill with a handful of tap water. He placed the bottle back and slammed the cabinet door. In the mirror, he saw Billy Darrell standing behind him.

Marcus swiveled around. No one was there. He took a deep breath and chalked it up to another hallucination, and went back to bed. He locked his bedroom door and put his head under the blankets, and when he had to relieve his bladder later he used a plastic bin for a chamber pot that he resolved himself to clean thoroughly the next morning. He didn't sleep much that night, and every time he heard a noise he buried himself deeper under the covers.

The next morning, Marcus got out of bed but the light of day didn't do much to dispel the feeling of dread that had encompassed him. He trundled downstairs, still missing his slippers. He searched and found them by the fireplace.

He didn't recall taking them off there, but there they were. He slipped his feet into them and shuffled into the kitchen, his eyes on the half-empty bottle of scotch. He'd been so proud of himself for having gone almost two years sober this time. It was a great feeling, that feeling of power. For the longest time he'd been able to stare at that bottle of scotch and not want a drink, but will power is a funny thing. Sometimes, the tiniest nudge can put the addiction back in control. Falling back into it was comforting on some levels, like spending time with an old friend. But it was also full of shame.

He could either make this day the first day on a new step to sobriety, or he could continue his descent off the wagon. He noticed the Stamden letter on the table, the trigger that had set this wagon fall in motion. He didn't remember leaving it on the table. He thought he'd brought it with him into the den, but he had been drinking the night before which meant anything could be anywhere.

Marcus sat down and tapped his fingers on the table. He picked up the letter and traced the return address with his finger.

He didn't want to move to a new residence again so soon. He'd only been here for a few weeks, not even three months, and it was all happening again. He'd hoped that getting sober was going to help, and it had for a while. This most recent move was supposed to help keep him sober, as there were too many triggers in his last place.

Five months was the shortest length he'd lasted in a home before he had to move, and it was getting more and more difficult the older he got. His parents had died long ago, and one by one his connections in this world were dying.

The Donation

Frederick Boyd passed away ten years after they graduated from Stamden. He was walking out of his office late one evening, and a pickup truck that was never identified careened for him. Frederick was hit from behind. He flipped over the truck and landed on the other side of the parking lot. The police never had any suspects; it was an unsolved hit-and-run.

Not long after Frederick's death, Marcus got a letter from Stamden. Over the years he'd received several donation requests from them, and most of the time he tossed them into a drawer. But after Frederick's death, he received a letter that wasn't like the others.

There was the typical purple and gold lettering, but on the return address it said "The Chancellor, Mumford Hall." He'd never received a donation request from the chancellor before, and thought it was odd. He opened the envelope. The letter was handwritten in large purple calligraphy.

Dear Mr. Adams,

In order for our progress to continue here at Stamden University, we greatly depend upon the bounty of former alumni such as yourself.

We are waiting patiently for your donation.

Most cordially,

Chancellor Jane Helsmoortel

The name was unfamiliar to Marcus. She was obviously new to Stamden's staff. It had been several years since he'd been there, of course there was new blood in the administration, and probably the faculty. But there was something about the surname Helsmoortel that gave Marcus a rush of gooseflesh.

After that letter arrived, Marcus began seeing Billy Darrell everywhere he went. He was in every mirror, every large window he walked by, and always in his dreams.

He thought he'd successfully blocked out what had happened, but after Frederick's death all of the memories of that day swarmed into his mind. No amount of scotch would completely block it out, so he tried changing environments.

Marcus moved to a new town and took a job at an investment firm owned by a friend of his father's. He didn't get another letter from Stamden for some time. Occasionally he touched base with James and Rand, but they never got together like they kept saying they would. Their phone conversations were often awkward. They never spoke of Frederick's death.

Marcus asked Rand once if he received any odd donation letters from Stamden. Rand said he'd gotten a few but always threw them away without opening them.

A couple of years after Frederick's death, James took his own life by jumping out of a twenty-two-story window. There wasn't any note, and the people in his life wouldn't describe him as depressed in any sense.

Marcus got another letter from the chancellor after he attended James's funeral. As soon as he saw the letter he gave notice at his job, packed up and moved to a different state. He was running out of favors to ask of his father's friends, and running out of money in his trust fund. He suspected it was around that time he made the switch to Dewar's.

When he decided to quit drinking after Rand's death and join a support group, he was not only ready to accept a higher power but almost ready to go home to it. Rand Tyson was mugged and killed in Manhattan late one evening.

He'd traveled there for a business trip, and no one knew why he'd been out so late, as the meeting he'd attended was over hours ago. Knowing Rand, Marcus suspected he was a late night caller for a lady friend and was accosted on his way home. He went to his first AA meeting soon after hearing the news.

Over the years he'd gone back and forth on sobriety, and this January he would've been sober for two years, the longest he'd ever gone without a drink. Sometimes he wondered what the point of it all was. He was dying anyway according to his doctor. There were moments when he wished that whatever fate lay ahead of him would just happen already, that whoever killed his friends would hurry up and kill him too, the sooner the better.

He thought about moving, but moving to a new city certainly hadn't helped him escape Stamden and those eerie donation letters. It certainly hadn't helped him stay sober, either. He'd been somewhat successful in conquering his demons before by confronting his alcoholism. Perhaps the only way to conquer the remaining demons would be to visit Stamden, bare his soul from the burden he'd been carrying, and give the donation they'd been asking for. After all, he was the last one left from that day. It seemed important to reveal to someone what had really happened, before it was too late for him to do so.

He picked up the phone and made the travel arrangements. When he hung up, he noticed his hands weren't trembling anymore. But they started trembling again when the day of his flight neared.

As soon as his plane landed, Marcus took a taxi to the Stamden campus. He sat in the back wringing his hands and his heartbeat quickened when they approached the school.

He expected to see students on the quad playing football or tossing Frisbees, co-eds sitting amongst the autumn leaves on the ground, but the campus was deserted. It filled him with chills, the bareness of it all.

He wondered why it was so empty, and then remembered it was Thanksgiving weekend. Most students would've traveled home for turkey and pie and wouldn't return until Sunday afternoon.

The taxi stopped at the main walkway that led up to Mumford Hall. Marcus got out of the backseat and held onto his wooden cane as he walked.

A young dark-haired man was riding the lawnmower across the quad. Marcus caught a glimpse of his face when he turned the mower around, and thought he was looking at a much older version of Billy Darrell.

As the man on the lawnmower got closer, Marcus focused on his face. He froze and gripped his cane, his knuckles white.

"It's him, it's Billy!" Marcus shouted without meaning to. The man on the mower stopped and stared at him.

"Can I help you?"

"I-I'm sorry," Marcus stuttered. "You looked like someone I knew."

The man on the mower shook his head, then turned and rode away. Marcus breathed evenly and kept walking.

He could've sworn that man was Billy. He looked exactly how Billy would look now.

He walked toward Mumford Hall where Jane Helsmoortel waited at the bottom of the stone steps. She had a shock of red hair that reminded him of Rand. She wore it short but shaggy and tucked behind her ears, the curled ends giving her a look of downturned horns.

"Mr. Adams, what a pleasure! We always enjoy meeting with alumni. Thank you for taking the time to come out on this holiday weekend."

"You're welcome."

He reached out and shook her outstretched hand. Either he was very cold, or she was very warm, as his hand seemed to melt into hers.

"I was curious," he said. "How did you find my new address? I hadn't alerted anyone that I'd moved, even the post office."

"Oh, I make it a point to keep track of all alumni. That's my job!"

She threw her hands up in the air and laughed. Her laugh was a big, loud guffaw that he wouldn't have expected to come out of a woman with her feminine features.

"If I didn't know how to get in touch with precisely every past student at this university, I'd be out of a job!" She winked at him.

Marcus didn't think she'd answered his question, but he didn't press her any further. She seemed to be one of those efficient, all-business people who took charge of conversations and he was too tired from his travels to keep up with her.

"Follow me this way!"

She turned and walked up the stairs, her red suede pumps clicking. She gestured at Marcus to follow, but he could not keep up with her. She already towered over him by half a foot and her legs seemed to make up half of her body height.

She reached the door and looked around for him with her eyebrows raised. Marcus was still puttering along with his cane, nearly out of breath. She opened the door and held it for him and waited with a smile plastered on her face.

"S-sorry," he said, feeling as if she should be the one apologizing for walking so quickly.

"No rush, Mr. Adams. Please take your time!"

Once they were inside she led him to her office decorated with mahogany furniture and plush velvet chairs.

"I like to make alumni feel…comfortable," Jane said and pulled out a chair. She gestured for Marcus to sit down.

As he sank into the chair he took notice of the carvings on the desk. It looked like faces with mouths wide open in moans, all entwined within dozens of other faces. Then he took a second look, and the faces were just grooves in the wood.

But when he looked again, they appeared to be moaning faces. He tore his eyes away and glanced up at Jane Helsmoortel. She was shoving papers across the desk at him.

"I took the liberty of drawing up the donation papers," she said with a wink.

Marcus sighed as he picked up the stack of papers. They felt warm.

"Hot off the printer!" She smiled.

He set them down and looked at her.

"Before I sign them, I wanted to tell you about something."

"Oh?"

"Something that happened here years ago, that I've always kept secret. I just...I feel the need to bare my soul of this."

"Of course!" Jane sat back and clasped her hands in her lap. "Please, do go on!"

"Well, it's about Billy Darrell."

"Billy who?"

"Billy Darrell, the son of the old groundskeeper. He used to go to school here."

"That's right, of course!" Jane snapped her fingers.

"So you've heard of him?"

"Yes, I have. As a matter of fact, our current groundskeeper is his brother!"

Marcus nearly jumped out of his seat.

"That's why he looked so familiar! I thought he was an older version of Billy Darrell. He nearly gave me a fright. I didn't know Billy had any siblings."

"Just the one. He was a baby when Billy went to school here."

"I see. Listen, Ms. Helsmoortel, what I have to say is...shocking, to say the least. I'm not sure if this is something you want Billy's family to be aware of, especially with the school's potential involvement."

"What do you mean, the school's potential involvement?"

Jane leaned forward in her chair, her eyes narrowed.

Marcus sighed.

"Please, for at least the time being, promise me that this conversation is between the two of us. I feel the need to bare my soul of this, before I...before..."

Marcus's voice cracked toward the end. He set his cane against Jane's desk and took a bottle of pills from his breast pocket. His hands shook the entire time and caused the pills in the bottle to shake.

Jane took in his yellowed face heightened by the overhead light in her office, and the way his hands trembled. A frown appeared on both her lip and brow.

"I'm so sorry, Mr. Adams. Yes, anything you say here will be between the two of us."

"Thank you."

As Marcus began he felt himself slipping into a slight stupor as his memory overcame him. Jane watched him as his eyes glazed over while he told his tale.

* * * * *

After the incident in the cafeteria, Frederick asked Marcus to meet him in the library at the end of classes. When they got there he pulled Marcus to a secluded cubicle in the corner.

"I'm ready to go ape shit on that feeb Billy Darrell," Frederick whispered. "But I want to do something that'll last, not something that'll heal like a swollen lip."

"Okay." Marcus's voice came out in a croak and he cleared his throat.

"I need your help. You're the smartest guy I know, and I'm hoping you'll come up with something good."

"I don't know…"

"Come on, you can think of something!"

"Maybe we could just tell people he has a small dong?" Marcus shrugged his shoulders. Frederick raised his eyebrows.

"That's the best you can come up with?"

The Donation

"Give me some time, I'll come up with something good."

Marcus didn't want to do anything to Billy Darrell, and wished Frederick would just let it go. But he also knew how much influence Frederick had with the Kappa Phi fraternity, and didn't want to get on his bad side. The next afternoon Marcus assembled James, Frederick and Rand in the library and told them his plan.

"First, we're going to make Billy think we want to make him an honorary Kappa Phi."

"What?" Frederick said.

"Just hear me out. Then, we're going to say he has to go through a special initiation, with just us, not the rest of the frat."

"Now you're talking!" Frederick clapped him on the back, and was shushed by the librarian. Marcus lowered his voice as he continued and the others leaned in closer.

"We'll get him to the lake, where he has to strip down to his birthday suit and jump into the water."

"Okay, what'll that do?" Frederick asked.

"Haven't you ever been in cold water before?"

"Yeah, so?"

"Haven't you ever noticed what happens in cold water?"

Frederick's round face brightened and his eyes widened. James snickered.

"Oh yeah, the ole shrinking dangle!" Rand nodded with a smile.

"Then what?" Frederick asked.

"I forgot to tell you the other part. We'll invite the cheerleaders down ahead of time, tell them to be there right around the same time Billy will be coming out of the water."

"That's not bad," Frederick said.

Jenna Moquin

"I think the toughest part will be getting him to think we want to be friends," Marcus said.

As it turned out, that part wasn't difficult at all. When Marcus approached Billy in the cafeteria and told him they were impressed with how he'd stood up to Frederick, and wanted him to join their frat as an honorary member, Billy practically tripped over himself thanking him. Marcus reminded himself of how slow Billy was in his classes, and squashed the pang of guilt that came over him with a nip from his flask.

Billy agreed to come to the lake just before the pep rally. Marcus told Rand and James to ask the cheerleaders to stop by the lake for a big surprise before they went off to the rally.

Marshpea Lake was more of a pond than a lake, and wasn't generally reserved for swimming. Just on the outskirts of campus, it was a decorative pond used by the school to have waterfront events during the warm weather. Most people never went into the water, though the Kappa Phi fraternity had made several pledges jump into the lake over the years.

Fifteen minutes before the pep rally Marcus, James, Frederick and Rand stood in a circle near a group of trees near Marshpea Lake. When Billy arrived they opened up the circle and had him join them inside it.

"William Darrell," Frederick said. "This is your honorary initiation into the Kappa Phi brotherhood. As a pledge, do you agree to do everything we tell you, no questions asked?"

"Yes, I do." Billy nodded.

"You say 'yes, I do, Sir!' Understand?"

"Yes, I do, sir!"

"Good. Now, strip and purify yourself in the waters of Marshpea Lake."

"What?"

"That sounds like a question!" Rand piped up.

"Sorry, sir, I just don't understand."

"You do as we say, you don't have to understand it!" Frederick said.

"I-I mean, I don't understand what you mean by purify yourself."

Rand stifled a laugh. James looked at Marcus.

"It means you have to get naked and take a dip in the lake, Billy," Marcus said in a leaden tone. He'd forgotten to bring his flask and was missing it at that moment.

"Oh, but isn't the water freezing?" Billy glanced at the lake with his eyebrows furrowed.

"You want to be in our frat, or not?" Frederick said. "A real man wouldn't be scared of a little cold water."

"It's just for a minute, Billy. We all had to do something like this during pledge week," Marcus said. He glanced in the direction of the path that led to the school. He hoped the cheerleaders arrived soon. He wanted to get this over with and go back to his room where he had a bottle of scotch waiting for him.

"It's true," Rand said. "I had to run naked through the football field at midnight."

"My old man got paddled back when he was pledging!" Frederick chimed in.

"Really?" Billy looked at Frederick.

"He's a Kappa Phi legacy, you know!"

Billy stared at the water. He was shaking all over.

"Go on then." Frederick nudged him.

"Are you sure no one can see me?"

"It's just us. Don't worry!" Frederick grinned.

Billy took off his jacket one sleeve at a time, then took a deep breath and undressed in just a few seconds. Frederick stared at him and laughed.

"I see why you're an expert on tiny dangles!"

"It's cold out here." Billy turned his back on them and walked toward the water. "You know what happens when it's cold."

"I'm counting on it, Lawnmower," Frederick said under his breath.

"Hey Freddy," Rand said once Billy was out of earshot. "Maybe he doesn't have to go all the way in, you know? It's so cold out here anyway, he probably doesn't even need to go in the water! I mean, it looked pretty small to me."

"I don't just want it small, I want it to shrink up the way it does in cold water!" Frederick looked at Billy, who was gingerly wading into the lake.

"Keep going! You have to completely dive in!" Frederick shouted at him.

Billy looked back at them, then at the lake. He took a deep breath, closed his eyes, and dove into the water.

"Rand, where are the girls?" Marcus looked toward the path, and the rest of the boys looked away from the lake.

"I don't know!" Rand shrugged. "James, what time did you tell them?"

James looked at him with his eyes widening larger by the second.

"I didn't talk to the girls, I thought you did!"

"Don't kid around, what time did you tell them?"

"I swear you said you were gonna tell them!"

"No Jimbo, I told you to!"

"Don't call me Jimbo! And I told you I had to study!"

"So the girls aren't coming at all?" Rand threw up his hands. "What a waste of time."

"The pep rally begins at five," Marcus said and looked at his watch. "It's already a few minutes past by now!"

Faintly in the distance they heard the band starting up the pep rally, and the cheerleaders hollering.

"Well, they're definitely not coming." Marcus turned back to the lake. "Where's Billy?"

His eyes searched the surface of the water and it was smooth with just a layer of foggy mist. He looked over at the pile of clothes Billy had left on the ground and glanced around the trees. Billy was nowhere to be seen.

"Billy?" Marcus took a step closer to the lake.

"Billy!" Frederick called out.

Marcus walked toward the edge of the water. James and Rand followed, stepping over Billy's clothes.

"Jesus H. Christ," Rand said, his voice shaking. "Did he just drown?"

"Oh my God!" James turned toward them. "Where is he?"

"Billy!" Frederick took a few steps into the lake, his shoes splashing water around him. "Stop fooling around now and come out!"

"How could he have drowned?" James said. "He hasn't been out there for long!"

"And wouldn't we have heard him struggling, splashing in the water?" Marcus said.

"I don't remember seeing him go into the water," James added. "But it's sort of foggy out here too. It's like he disappeared!"

"Maybe he's just swimming and can't hear us," Frederick said.

"He's not swimming you moron!" Marcus felt like screaming. "Do you know how cold that water is?"

"What if he didn't even know how to swim?" James said.

"He wouldn't have gone in there if he didn't!" Frederick said. "He's not that stupid!"

"But what if he is?" Marcus said. "What if he is that stupid? He isn't exactly on the dean's list."

"What do we do?" Rand sniffled.

"Maybe we should try to find him. What if he just got a cramp or something and needs help out there?"

"Who's gonna do it?" Rand asked.

"It was your idea, Marcus," Frederick said.

"Don't try to pin this on me, Boyd!" Marcus spat. "You're the one who wanted to get back at him."

"But you came up with this stupid idea!"

"Ten minutes ago you loved this idea." Marcus didn't argue anymore as he stripped down to his underwear and waded into the lake.

"Billy! Billy where are you?" The water was so cold Marcus felt like he was walking into a giant bucket of ice. His teeth chattered and his eyes watered. He half dove in a breaststroke, sucking in air as the cold water seized his veins and heart. He kept his head above the water as he treaded it, and had trouble seeing with the thickening fog.

"Billy!" His voice was growing hoarse. He felt something graze his leg and gasped, then coughed. He eased his leg movement and tried to be as still as possible and felt it again. Something, or someone was grabbing at his ankle.

Marcus almost swallowed a mouthful of lake water as he dunked his head. He reached down to his ankles and felt something slimy and stringy. He went back up to the surface for a gulp of air and went under again.

He opened his eyes and ignored the sting, but still couldn't see well in the murky water. He felt around rows and rows of various plant life growing out of the bottom of the lake. The vines were intertwined, like slimy ropes. He sifted through the vines thinking Billy was caught in them, but had to keep going back to the surface for air.

The realization of what had happened to Billy washed over him in a chill that was colder than the water he was in. He swam back to the boys waiting for him, shaking his head as he shivered into his clothes. He told them about the vines.

"He must've gotten caught up in those vines, if he wasn't a strong swimmer," James said and hung his head. He muttered to himself and wiped his cheeks. He paced back and forth between the trees.

"Holy smokes, guys, I can't...I just can't..." Rand didn't bother wiping away the tears running down his face. "We told him to purify himself. We told him to jump in."

"I'm never gonna forgive myself for this." Marcus dry heaved, but his stomach was completely empty and nothing came up. He felt the urge to vomit all over the ground, but nothing came out. That sick feeling stayed inside of him, and he thought at the time he'd be able to sate it with some scotch. He had no idea that feeling would be with him in a subtle way for the rest of his life, an underlying coat of sickness that would always be there to remind him of this.

"It's not your fault." Frederick, the only one of them who seemed calm, patted Marcus on the back. "It's none of our faults. We didn't do anything wrong."

"What?" James looked at him.

"We didn't know he couldn't swim!" Frederick threw his hands up in the air.

"Are you crazy?" Marcus coughed and pulled his jacket tighter around himself.

"Listen, how many of us have jumped into that lake and were fine?"

Marcus tilted his head. James sighed and Rand nodded.

"Dozens of us, right?" Frederick continued. "None of us ever checked to see if we were strong swimmers or not, did we? No, we just jumped in! Any one of us could've drowned and we didn't, which makes this nothing but a case of bad luck."

Marcus was still shaking, but the thought Frederick had put into his head gave him an odd sort of comfort. It was a freak accident, something that could've happened to any pledge. The sick feeling in his stomach dulled. It didn't go away, but it was dulled.

"Well, what do we do now?" James asked. "Should we report this to the police, or the school?"

"Report what?" Frederick said. "I say we just walk away, pretend we were never here."

"What?" James and Rand said in unison.

"Someone will report him missing," Frederick looked at the lake and tapped his chin while he spoke. "They'll go searching for him, and they'll probably check the lake. They'll find his body and say he either committed suicide, or went for a dip and drowned."

"In this weather?" Marcus crossed his arms over his chest.

"Fine, then they'll say he killed himself."

"But why would he take his clothes off to do it?"

"I don't know!" Frederick was shouting. He cupped his hands and blew into them.

"He committed suicide, he's crazy!" Frederick said. "Who knows why he stripped? Just stay clear of his clothes so they don't look tampered with."

"Fine. Agreed. Let's get out of here," Marcus said. He stuffed his hands into his pockets and walked up the path. He didn't look behind to see if the rest of them were following him, but they were.

Frederick was worried they'd look suspicious if they didn't attend the pep rally so they all went. Marcus insisted on stopping by the frat house to change his wet clothes, but what he really wanted to do was pick up his flask.

He hid it under his jacket and met the rest of them outside. He secretly drank from it during the walk there, and felt the wonderfully comforting sensation of uncaring run through him.

They sat through the rally, and the football game that followed. The only one who seemed able to keep a smile on his face was Frederick.

It was a few days before anyone noticed Billy was missing. His supervisor from the cafeteria reported it when Billy didn't show up for two shifts in a row, and no one had seen him around campus. They called the police, and that was when they found his clothes near the lake, and searched it for his body. They never found it.

Franklin Boyd, Frederick's father, donated $100,000 to the school later that year, and Stamden built a new football stadium. Marcus and the rest of them vowed to never speak of what happened.

Rand began dating a bunch of different girls, and he didn't spend much time at the frat house. James was never around either, always studying or having tutoring sessions with Professor Galen. Frederick ended up joining the football team, and hung out with his new teammates more often than his frat brothers. Marcus found his comfort in emptying a tumbler of scotch, reading a good book and getting lots of sleep.

* * * * *

Marcus sat back in his chair and looked at Jane Helsmoortel. She tapped her long red fingernails against the desk blotter, her right eyebrow raised.

"Well?" she said. "Is that all?"

"No." He sighed and told her how his friends began dying one by one, beginning with Frederick.

"And I'm the last one."

"The last one?"

"Unless dying slowly counts. Billy's death did start me drinking more heavily than I ever had before."

Jane shuffled the donation papers and opened a drawer. She pulled out a large black binder.

"I'm going to have you sign another document along with these. Just a little something that states the school had no involvement in Billy's demise."

"You know, they never found his body." Marcus looked at the carpet. "They combed that lake for two days…it wasn't a big lake, a pond really. But they never found his body. I always found that strange. But he must've drowned. There's no other explanation!"

"Unless something ate him."

"Ate him?"

She nodded.

"What could've been living in the pond?" Marcus raised his eyebrows.

"One never knows with wildlife. I'm always hearing about fish or reptiles, indigenous to certain areas suddenly showing up out of character in spots they didn't think it could inhabit."

The Donation

"I doubt something large enough to eat a grown person was living in that lake."

"Just a thought. Piranha? Maybe flesh-eating bacteria?"

"I suppose you have a point." Marcus shrugged. "Though my imagination does get the better of me sometimes. When I first walked up to the campus and saw the groundskeeper, I could've sworn it was Billy! And my first thought was how they never found his body."

"Well he is related to him, so I'm sure that's where you saw the resemblance."

"Do you think I should tell Billy's brother what really happened, or will you do me that favor?"

"Oh, I think it's best if you leave here after signing these papers and making your donation to Stamden, and never speaking of this again, to anyone. We wish you the best of luck, Mr. Adams."

She shoved the papers across the desk at him. Marcus sighed and picked up an old-fashioned fountain pen from the cup holder. He signed each page where she'd marked with a little red flag. After he signed the last one, Marcus put down the pen.

"Hmm, wait a minute," Jane said as she rummaged around the desk. "There's one more. Ah! If it had been a snake it would've bitten me."

She winked at him.

"This is the last one, the most important one in fact. This form states that the donation you're making is a binding contract, one that cannot be terminated. You do understand, Mr. Adams? Once you sign, and make this donation, it cannot be undone."

Marcus picked up the pen. Jane Helsmoortel stared at him with her big amber eyes. The gaze was so intense, her eyes appeared to be glowing.

While he signed he felt a chill that traveled up his spine to the back of his head, and he shuddered. He wished he was sitting next to his fireplace with a good book and a glass of scotch. He looked at his watch. As long as he caught his flight in time, he would be soon.

"I already understood that. You people like being dramatic, don't you?"

"What do you mean by you people?"

"Redheads." Marcus tossed the contract across the desk at her. Jane laughed.

"It's been a pleasure doing business with you, Mr. Adams."

"Now, is that all?"

"Yes. You're free to go."

Marcus stood up with the creaks of his joints quite audible, picked up his cane and gave Jane Helsmoortel one last look.

"Thank you for letting me bare my soul to you."

"You're welcome, Mr. Adams." She nodded. "I'm sure it made this donation so much easier."

Marcus nodded at her and left the room. He kept an eye out for the groundskeeper, Billy's brother, but didn't see him or the lawnmower. He made it to the taxi Jane had called for him, and stared at the school while they drove off toward the airport.

Either it was the fog settling, or his eyes were unfocused, but the campus appeared to fade in and out as the taxi drove away. When he blinked it came back into focus, and then he could no longer see Stamden as the taxi rounded the corner.

When Marcus arrived home he poured himself a drink. He'd gone back to Lagavulin. He figured if he was going to do something wrong, he should at least do it right.

He went into the den and sat by the fireplace. It had been a long plane ride, and baring his soul hadn't made him feel as good as he thought it would. He was hoping it would make that feeling in his stomach go away, but he didn't feel any different. He looked at the photograph of him, James, Frederick and Rand, and raised his glass in a toast to them.

"Here's to you, my friends."

He tilted his head back and downed the glass. He closed his eyes, savoring the hum of the elixir in his body as it coursed through to the tips of his fingers. It was moments like this when Marcus wondered why he would ever want to stop drinking.

His front door shook with heavy knocking. Marcus gripped his cane and pulled himself out of the chair. Twilight had settled and the house was dimmer than it had been moments ago. He reached over to the light switch and flipped it up, but no light came on.

His hands began trembling. He looked toward the front door and saw movement through the small window on top. The knock came again, only much softer, and the front porch creaked. Marcus stood still and waited, and hoped whoever was there would assume no one was home, and leave.

After a few moments, the knocking ceased and he no longer heard creaks from the front porch. He inched his way to the front door and looked up at the window. He couldn't see anything, so he went to the windows in the living room that overlooked the porch. No one was there. Marcus breathed a sigh and went back to the den. He poured himself another scotch and finished it in a few seconds.

The penetratingly shrill sound of breaking glass came from the living room, startling him. Marcus grabbed his cane and headed toward the noise. He inched closer. The large middle window overlooking the porch had been shattered. A dark figure stood near it.

"Hello Marcus." The voice that came out was low and gravelly.

Marcus focused on the shape. It looked like the groundskeeper from Stamden.

"Aren't you Billy Darrell's brother?"

He didn't respond. He had an earthy aroma that Marcus assumed came with the job of being a groundskeeper.

"Why did you break my window?"

"You wouldn't open the door."

"But…but what are you doing here?"

"It's time, Marcus."

"What do you mean?"

"It's your time. You're the last one on my list."

"Your list?"

"First I took care of Frederick, that smug bastard."

Marcus shivered. He exhaled and his breath made a cloud. The air in the room was growing colder by the second. His hands shook harder than ever, and he dropped his cane.

"He wasn't difficult at all. None of you were."

He took a step closer. Marcus felt his bowels cramp up. He wished wholeheartedly that this was just another hallucination. A vivid, horrifying hallucination.

"James really wanted to die, I think. As soon as he saw me, he threw himself out of that window. I didn't even have to do much!"

"It was you! You killed them, you sick, evil…"

"Me? What about what you all did? Are you kidding me?"

"What we did to Billy was an accident, a prank gone wrong! What you're doing is intentional, in revenge for your brother!"

"My brother?"

He laughed. Marcus grew short of breath and there was a tingling sensation in his left arm, and a strange tightening in his chest. It felt like an icy hand was squeezing his heart. He clutched at his chest.

"You were right the first time you saw me, Marcus. I am Billy Darrell!"

He grabbed the cane from the floor. Marcus watched in horror as he lurched back and then swung it at his head. The cane came at him in a 3-D visual and his life flashed before his eyes. He saw his friends from Kappa Phi, a bottle of Lagavulin and the first time he got laid. The last thing he saw as the cane collided with his forehead was Billy's face as he waded into Marshpea Lake.

He fell to the floor as the dark figure slinked out of the room. Marcus twitched a couple of times on the carpet, then remained still.

A few days later Marcus's neighbor noticed a strange smell coming from his house. He knocked and there was no answer, and all of his curtains were drawn. He reported it to the police, who found Marcus's body in the living room, his cane on the floor next to him.

The cause of death was a heart attack according to the coroner. There was also blunt trauma to his head that matched the shape of his cane. The police determined that Marcus must have dropped his cane during the heart attack, and hit his head on it when he fell. They had searched and didn't find any signs of a break-in, anywhere in the house.

Jenna Moquin

The only noteworthy things they found were a half-empty bottle of scotch, and a fuzzy black and white photograph of four young men wearing matching sweaters.

Safe

Matt and Dana jogged along a chain-link fence searching for a new place to hide. Dana spotted an apartment building a block away. Most of the apartments had fire escapes with attached ladders so they wouldn't work. The more ways to get in, the less safe they were.

There were two apartments on the left side that were missing fire escapes: the top corner and the one directly beneath it.

"There," she said and pointed toward the building. Matt nodded.

They simultaneously looked left and right as they crossed the street, and hoped no one spotted them enter the building.

They trotted up the stairwell to the apartment, and their eyes darted at every corner. Matt tried the doorknob but it was locked. He shoved against it with his shoulder and winced.

"Let's try kicking it," Dana said.

They backed up a foot, and on the count of three stomped against the door with their feet. It didn't open, but they heard an encouraging creaking sound. They tried twice more before the door finally gave and burst open, still teetering on its hinges.

"Okay." Matt hustled her inside. "Keep lookout by the door. I'll check out the rest of the place. If you hear something just yell and I'll come running. Got it?"

Dana nodded. She chewed on her lip and kept her ears perked by the door. Matt gripped the buck knife that had become his prized tool these last few weeks and walked into the apartment.

In the next hallway were three doors, the middle one ajar showing the bathroom. He assumed the other doors were bedrooms, and chose the first one.

It appeared to be the master bedroom with a queen-size bed and mirrored closet. He slid the closet door open with his foot. There were a few items of clothing amongst many empty hangers. Next to the bed was a large umbrella. He picked it up and swished the clothes around in the closet. He believed whoever lived in this apartment had abandoned it, but he always checked the hiding spots, just to be safe.

He went to the next room, which had belonged to a child. There was a bed in the shape of a race car, baseball bats on the curtains, and the walls were painted light blue. The toy box in the corner had a few discarded items: a teddy bear with a missing arm, a plastic truck with no back tires, and a couple of bags of marbles.

"Whoever lived here took off so we're good to go," Matt said when he came back to the front door. He grinned, and Dana managed a small smile in return.

"What do we do about the door?"

He looked at the door. There was a chain lock, and the hinges were still fairly intact even after their forced entry.

"Let me look around for a hammer and some nails. Maybe I'll break off some dresser drawers and use them to board up the door. In the meantime, let's chain-lock it and put something heavy against it."

He knew a chain lock wouldn't do much. It was like a Band-Aid over a bruise. Sometimes you just needed it for comfort.

They shimmied a tall bookcase over to the door and then set about their tasks. Dana wanted to ransack the kitchen to see if any food was left behind. They'd found a pack of bottled water in the back of a liquor store the week prior so they'd had plenty of water, but they hadn't had much to eat lately.

She swept through the kitchen cabinets and wasn't disappointed with what she found. Cans of chicken noodle soup, a box of oyster crackers, an opened bag of pretzels with a plastic clip keeping the package tight, a jar of peanut butter with about a quarter left in it, and a couple of packets of Gummi bears.

In the pantry, she found an entire case of ginger ale, and her mouth watered at the sight of the shiny green cans. They weren't soda drinkers, but any beverage that wasn't water would be a treat.

Matt came into the kitchen after checking the rest of the apartment. He hadn't found any tools, and looked under the sink. Next to some cleaning products was a small safe. He tried to open it but it was locked.

"Lucky for us this safe has a lock, not a code to open it. See any keys around?" He looked up at Dana who was chewing with a guilty look on her face.

"I found food," she said, crumbs of pretzel flying out of her mouth. "I was just checking to make sure they weren't too stale."

Matt chuckled and took a pretzel from the bag. He kissed her on the forehead and surveyed the food she'd gathered on the counter.

"Awesome. I want to secure the front door, and then we can have a feast."

Dana helped him search for a key to the safe. They checked all of the kitchen drawers and found a few keys. None of them worked.

Matt found the key he was looking for in the master bedroom. It was taped to the bottom of the lamp on the nightstand.

Inside the safe was a metal toolbox. There was a hammer and saw among other tools, and a small plastic bin with mismatched nails and screws.

"Why would someone lock up their tools?" He asked Dana when she came back to the kitchen after taking her own tour of the apartment.

"I saw a little kid's room. Maybe they kept the tools locked up just to be safe."

"Good point."

Matt collected the dresser drawers from the bedrooms. He sawed off the fronts of the drawers and then hammered them to the door.

Dana drooled over the soft bed and pillows in the master bedroom. It felt like years since they'd slept in a bed. She was more excited over the sleep they were going to get that night than the ginger ale they were going to have with dinner.

She felt safe in this place, four stories up, with no way of getting in or out besides the door Matt had boarded up. Soon it would get dark, and they would be sure to keep the lights off and their movements to a minimum.

They ate a few more pretzels and three Gummi bears apiece. After splitting a can of soda, they heard a gunshot from outside. Dana sighed and her head fell to her chest, and a tear traveled down her cheek. Matt tipped up her chin with his hand and brushed the tear away.

"Don't worry. We'll get through this. We always do."

He always said that when times were tough, from late mortgage payments to her lay-off two years ago. He leaned in and kissed her. She kissed him back with such fervor he felt himself getting hard, but didn't imagine she would be in the mood. He was pleasantly surprised when she nodded toward the master bedroom and he picked her up and carried her to the bed.

Dana peeled off her clothes, hoping the lack of showering over the past few weeks wouldn't turn him off. Evidently it didn't as he went down on her the second her panties were on the floor.

She wrapped her legs around his head and stroked his hair with a deep moan. A few moments later, she rolled Matt over and returned the favor with the same fervor she'd kissed him with earlier. When she mounted him he grasped her backside and thrust deep into her.

Afterward, they fell asleep in each other's arms. When Dana woke up night had fallen.

"Shit!" She snapped and jumped up from the bed. "We forgot to close the shade!"

Matt was jolted awake. He watched through the window as a sedan on the street below was lit on fire. He yanked down the window shade, hoping that anyone who might have noticed them was distracted by the burning car. They hurried through the rest of the apartment making sure the curtains and shades were closed.

"Don't worry," Matt said. "I doubt anyone saw us."

Dana nodded and took a deep breath. They crept toward the window to peer outside at the fire.

Surrounding the burning car was a group of men, all bare-chested and ragged-looking. Matt pulled her away from the window and brought her back to bed. He held her close and wrapped the blanket around them. As Dana drifted off, she heard a woman screaming in the distance.

It took Matt longer to fall asleep. The sound of the woman's screams stayed with him for a while. He felt somewhat secured in the new hideout they'd found. As long as they didn't bring attention to themselves no one would know they were here, and hopefully the government and military would get everything straightened out soon. He wanted nothing more than to make his wife feel safe again.

Over the next few days, they acted like they were on a relaxing vacation. They slept a lot and played with the marbles from the toy box. They invented a game with the Gummi bears as a way to ration them, combined with Rock, Paper, Scissors. The best three out of five got to pick which body part of the Gummi bear the other got to eat: the feet, the head, or just nip off the ears, which was just a roundabout way of biting off the head.

Every once in a while they heard screams, or a gunshot, and at one point they heard a woman scream so loud it sounded like it was right next door. One afternoon, after they shared a cold can of soup, Dana rummaged through her backpack to find one of the few items she'd salvaged from their house. It was her favorite wedding photo inside a monogrammed frame. A close-up angle of their smiling faces, and they were looking into each other's eyes instead of the camera. Dana traced Matt's face with her forefinger.

She thought about their wedding day, and how she had pictured their life together. Kids, a big house with a yard, Christmases, and Halloween costumes. That future seemed impossible now. She felt a lump in her throat and tears in her eyes. Then her eyebrows shot up and she rushed into the kitchen. She opened up the safe underneath the sink.

Safe

She placed their wedding photo next to the hammer, and locked the safe. For a moment she kept her hand on top of the safe, and shuddered.

Matt walked into the kitchen and put his arm around her.

"Do you think life will ever go back to the way it was?" She looked at him.

"I don't know." Matt stared at the wall as he spoke to her. "Maybe it will. We'll just have to wait and see."

He pulled her closer to him and squeezed.

"We'll get through this," Matt whispered. "We always do."

Dana smiled at him, and he kissed her. She hoped if things ever went back to normal they could try having a family. She'd picture it whenever Matt held her. She'd close her eyes and see them with their kids, a boy and a girl, pushing them on swings, laughing and smiling.

She couldn't shake the feeling that time was slipping away from them. She knew they would eventually run out of food, and wasn't sure what would happen then.

They went to the bedroom and went underneath the blanket, though all they did was hold each other. They held each other for so long they drifted into a deep sleep, and night fell around them.

They had left the bedside table lamp on earlier. Even though the shade was half-drawn, the light shined a beam onto the dark street below. When Dana woke up she noticed the light and jolted out of bed. In her haste to turn off the lamp she knocked it over, then rushed over to the window. Matt followed her.

She peered outside. On the ground below stood a row of five bulky men wielding guns and crowbars. The one in the middle pointed up at her. They began chanting and pumping their weapons up and down.

She jumped back from the window but she knew it was too late. They'd been spotted. Matt ran to the front door checking the security of the boards. They suddenly looked a lot weaker than they did when he'd first boarded up the door.

Dana was behind him, and they heard the men running up the stairs, hollering as they got closer. Her eyes widened as she looked at her husband. Matt glanced around at the side table by the door.

"Maybe we could put something up against it?"

Dana shook her head at him and her shoulders slumped. She began to tremble.

They heard the pounding against the door and the floor beneath them shook.

"No!" Matt slammed his fist against the boards. "Stay the hell out!"

Dana put her hands on his shoulders and pressed her forehead against the back of his neck.

"It's useless Matt. They're just going to kill you. What they're going to do to me is so much worse."

He turned around and put his arms around his wife. As he felt her shudder in his arms he stroked her hair with one hand.

With his other hand, he reached around to the side table where he kept his buck knife. He clicked the blade out and pulled away from her.

"I wanted nothing more than to make you feel safe again."

Tears fell from his eyes as the pounding continued against the door. Dana looked into his eyes with tears of her own. Matt reached up with the blade of the buck knife facing her. The realization of what he meant to do hit Dana. Her heart thudded in her chest and she gasped.

"I love you," Matt said as he brought the blade down. Just before it reached her throat, Dana whispered "I love you, too."

The blade sliced through her throat at the very last word. Blood oozed down her neck and she collapsed into his arms as the men broke through the door. Three of the men pulled Matt away and held him back, while two of them grabbed Dana and took off with her, whooping and hollering. One of the men gripped Matt's head and twisted it until his neck snapped.

The men who'd taken Dana didn't realize she was dead until they got outside. They were already covered in so much blood, they hadn't noticed any more of it.

Jenna Moquin

Waiting Room

Waiting rooms always look the same to me. Totally generic with a lame attempt at being cheerful with light colors on the walls. At least this waiting room had a TV. I hate the ones that just have magazines and board games.

I sat there with a cup of coffee in my hand, waiting to hear if Devin was going to be okay. When we first got here cops were everywhere, but not so much now. I remember following the paramedics when they wheeled him in from the ambulance. His hand was hanging off the stretcher so I reached down and grabbed it.

"Andy?" He coughed.

"Just be cool, Dev," I told him to be cool, even though I wasn't. At all.

He was the only one who ever called me Andy. It was our thing. Everyone else called me Drew. It started with Mom. She said the end of Devin's name and the beginning of mine both sound like the word "and" so it's quicker to say "Dev & Drew!"

He was always first. He was the first born, eleven months older than me. He was the first to walk, the first to learn the backstroke, the first to hit a baseball, the first to kiss a girl.

Mom and I stood there waiting for someone to tell us what was next. A woman in scrubs came up and introduced herself as Nurse Tracey. She told Mom they may have to transfer Dev to the hospital in Seattle depending on how bad his injuries were. A guy in scrubs that I assumed was the doctor, or maybe another nurse wheeled him away.

There were cops all over the place. I didn't realize Devin Mathers getting totaled was such big news. He's a popular guy, and this is a football town, but cops? Come on.

"Why are the police here?" Mom asked.

"Oh, they caught the Green River Copycat Killer. He was injured during the police chase."

"Good God, is he here?" Mom's eyebrows shot up and she looked at Nurse Tracey.

The Green River Copycat Killer had gone uncaught for almost two years. They'd found four bodies so far. Only two of them had been found in the river, but they were calling him a copycat killer because of how he was murdering his victims. I hadn't been following it that much since it wasn't exactly fun stuff to think about.

"Don't worry Mrs. Mathers," Nurse Tracey said, and touched my mom's arm. She had a nice way about her. "They've got him handcuffed to the bed and he's being guarded. I think they're waiting for the FBI to show up, at least that's what the sheriff told me."

"The sheriff is here?"

"Yes, she was involved in the capture."

"Why can't they put him in jail? They must have doctors for prisoners!"

"Mom…" I nudged her shoulder.

"We're the only hospital in a thirty-mile radius. We still have to treat him, like any other patient."

Mom shook her head at me and rolled her eyes. I knew what that look meant. It meant that she wasn't getting her way, and she was pissed about it, but couldn't do anything about it.

I saw that same look after Dad came home with a new set of titanium golf clubs. Mom thought they should've agreed on what to spend his holiday bonus on and they argued for a while. Dad said he was the one who made the money so he could spend it how he wanted. The person she'd rolled her eyes at that time was Dad.

"Mom, where is Dad by the way?"

"I told you already. He had a meeting in Spokane, but he should be on his way back by now. I've been trying to get him on his cell but it keeps going straight to voice mail. He must not be getting any reception again."

My dad's company, I'm always forgetting what he does. It's either investments in properties or property management, or both. It's this huge company and they have another office in Spokane. Once in a while, my Dad has to travel there for a meeting.

Mom got us cups of coffee and we went to the waiting room. I wished Dad would call soon. He never usually missed one of Devin's games. He always sat between me and Mom in the third row of the bleachers. But tonight I hadn't given much thought to Dad not being there, because Cerie Verrier was sitting next to me in the bleachers.

Cerie Verrier had just transferred to our school from Vancouver. She had the most gorgeous golden hair I'd ever seen. Brown eyes, not blue. Dev noticed her first, of course. He does everything first. And at first I thought she liked him. Until tonight, when she came up to me right before the game.

"Hey Drew," she said. I didn't even know she knew my name.

"Hey," I said back. It was all I could say, because for a second I forgot what her name was. That's not good.

"Can I sit with you at the game tonight?"

She said it like it was something we did all the time. Like she wasn't the newest hot girl in school and every guy wanted her. And she asked me, not the other way around. I liked that.

"Uh, sure."

I knew I didn't have an extra seat. The games are always packed, and my parents would be there. But I figured if anyone would give up their seat for me, it would be Dad. And when Mom told me he couldn't make it that night, I didn't even listen to the reason why. I was so happy to have Cerie Verrier sitting next to me at the game. In the third row. Where everyone could see us.

And then Dev went down at the start of the second quarter. I don't know who the other guy was from Mount Si who tackled him, but it was two seconds after he caught the toss and Dev went down hard. The other guy was pretty big.

The funny thing was, right before he got hit I got this flash of us growing up together. We were running in the backyard, then we were jumping into the lake together, and then suddenly he was down. I had tunnel vision after that until we got him into an ambulance and to the hospital. All I could see was him. On that stretcher.

I heard Mrs. Cooper's voice nearby and looked up. She lives across the street from me, and she was talking to one of the cops. Our town only has like four cops, and according to my dad only two of them are competent.

Mrs. Cooper was talking to Sheriff Monet, who my dad considers one of the competent ones. She came here from Louisiana a couple of years ago after Sheriff Lane retired. It was the first time our town had a woman for a sheriff, and it made her pretty popular.

"I'm telling you, I saw the killer in my backyard tonight, right before he was captured!"

Mrs. Cooper moved her hands around as she spoke to the sheriff. She does that a lot. Whenever she comes over to complain that me and Dev are being too loud in the yard, I swear she's gonna fly away with how fast her hands are flapping around.

"What did he look like, Mrs. Cooper?" Sheriff Monet glanced at her phone as she spoke.

"Well, he had brown shaggy hair, he was about five foot ten, and broad shoulders…and he had a limp."

I looked at Mrs. Cooper. She could've been talking about Dad with that description. He got that limp after he fell during a hike up Mount Rainier and broke his foot.

"Did you get a look at his face?" Sheriff Monet asked. I wanted to hear this too so I inched closer to them.

"No, I just saw the back of him." Mrs. Cooper sighed and shook her head.

"All right, well thank you. We'll be in touch if we need any more."

Sheriff Monet walked out of the waiting room. I watched her leave and then walked over.

"Hi, Mrs. Cooper."

"Oh, hello Drew. How are you holding up? Any news about your brother?"

"Not yet. I heard you talking to the sheriff. You saw the killer they caught in your backyard tonight?"

"Yes, I did!" She nodded.

"How do you know it was the same guy they caught?"

"I saw him in the yard, snooping around. I was about to call the police when I heard sirens nearby. It was like my prayers had been answered! I wanted to call the police, and suddenly there they were!"

I shrugged, wishing she would get to the point.

"The man in my backyard panicked as soon as the sirens got closer, and he raced out! Moments later I heard on the news that they'd captured the copycat killer a few blocks down from my place."

I had to admit, it sounded good. But maybe it was just some regular burglar in her yard, since he would freak at the sound of sirens too. It's not like this town is crawling with burglars, though.

There was thunder outside, then rain hitting against the windows. I wondered if the game was over, or if they had to stop for the thunderstorm.

I took a sip of my coffee and it was cold, so I tossed it into the trash. Mom was arguing with Nurse Tracey. I went over to try and pull her away. That's when I saw Cerie Verrier walk in.

She was shaking out an umbrella. She looked around the waiting room, and her eyes stopped on me. My heart stopped beating for a second. She walked up to me.

"Drew, is Devin okay?"

"We don't know yet."

"How are you doing?"

She touched my arm. I felt so weird. I was worried about Dev, but I was also floating. I felt a big shit-eating grin about to show up on my face but we were in the hospital. My brother was injured, I had to look serious. It took a lot to keep that grin inside.

"I'm okay. Just worried 'bout Dev."

"Of course! He took a hard tackle tonight. How did he seem?"

I couldn't tell, but I thought I saw something in her eyes when she asked about Dev. Did she like him more than me, and was only pretending to be interested in me to get closer to my brother?

"He seemed pretty out of it, but I'm hoping it's just a broken leg or something."

"Well that's no fun, but it could be worse." I couldn't tell if she was into him more. She just seemed genuinely concerned about the whole situation. That made me like her even more.

We got coffee, and although I knew another cup would make me hyper I didn't want to get decaf. I wanted to show Cerie Verrier I was tough, so I got regular. I figured I'd take little sips.

Mom was on her phone, maybe she was trying to get a hold of Dad again. She kept dialing and then taking the phone away from her ear and shaking her head.

"Mom, can we see Dev?" I asked after she put the phone into her bag.

"I don't know, let me ask the nurse." Mom walked off toward the reception area. Cerie moved closer to me and rubbed my back.

"I'm so sorry this happened to your brother. You poor thing, I can't imagine how you must feel."

I didn't know what to say, but I wanted her to keep rubbing my back. It felt so good.

"Thanks."

She stopped rubbing but kept her hand in the middle of my back. The double glass doors slid open and in walked a group from our school. I could see the red and gold Cedar Point High jackets. The "rich kids" as Dev called them, the ones who lived in the hilly part of town and invited him to parties because he was the star quarterback. Even though we lived on the flat side of town.

They came in with some of the football players. They were slapping high-fives, and shaking out the big sorts of umbrellas that golfers use. It seemed like we won the game against Mount Si High.

"Hey, Cerie!" Joey Venereaux called out. He was the fullback on the team. I hated him.

"Hi," Cerie said and waved at him. She winked at me and then tossed her coffee into the nearest trash.

"Thanks for coming by. And the coffee." I held up the coffee and winked. She smiled again. Damn that smile was amazing.

"You're welcome." She gave me this cute little half wave and walked over to Joey. I sat down, torn between being worried about Dev and thinking about Cerie and Joey.

A woman with two little girls rushed into the waiting room. The girls were crying and calling the woman "Auntie" so I guessed she was their aunt.

"Mommy's going to be fine. She just has to get some medicine and the doctor will fix her up and then we can go home!"

The girls nodded at Auntie, but didn't look like they believed her. One of the girls had red, white and blue ribbons in her hair. It reminded me of the Fourth of July, and I thought back to when we went to the beach for the Fourth last summer.

Dev and I went off exploring on the rocks. The tide had been high the night before and left lots of debris all over the rocks. Dev walked ahead of me. I could smell the saltiness in the air, and a couple of seagulls flew by. The waves smashed up against the rocks and he let out a whistle.

"Andy, come over here!" He waved me over. He crouched down as he looked at something by his feet.

I walked over and my feet slipped on the rocks. Some of them were jagged and dug into my toes, but I kept moving forward until I got to where he was pointing. I didn't see anything but wet rocks.

Then he pointed it out. It was a hand. I jumped back and slipped on the rocks, and he caught me before I fell.

"I think it was a woman," he said. I think he was right, between the ring and the nail polish. Well, the nail polish that was still there, on the fingers that were still there. I wanted to throw up. But I also wanted to show Dev I was as tough as he was. I swallowed back what the nasty burp brought up.

We told Dad about it. He came over with us and looked at the hand. He told us to leave it, and then we left to go home. Dad said not to tell anyone. But I don't remember if he ever called the cops to tell them. I didn't hear anything about it, and then we went on a trip to Wild Waves and I forgot all about the hand.

After sitting around the waiting room for a while, I didn't know what to do. Joey Venereaux had Cerie cornered, and a couple of the cheerleaders were getting coffee with the football players.

The TV in the waiting room was playing the news. I hated watching the news. It was too damn depressing, and life was depressing enough as it was. Did they have to throw it in our faces all the time?

The magazines were stacked inside this rack on the wall. Never was a big reader, but maybe there was something in there better than the news.

There wasn't, really. Just *National Geographic* and *Cosmopolitan*. No *Sports Illustrated*, I was shocked, seeing as this was such a football town. But maybe someone swiped it.

Waiting Room

I walked around the waiting room. There was another TV across the room. It was a different station, but still the news. This one was showing a story about the Green River Copycat Killer. The one who was here in the hospital.

The cops had him handcuffed in a room here somewhere. I hadn't been paying much attention to the story, but since the killer was in the same building I figured I should know more about him. I sat down to watch the news report on him.

They called him a copycat killer because he was killing prostitutes in the same manner as the original serial killer, Gary Ridgway. After having sex with them, he strangled them and tossed them into the river. This guy though, according to the news, had only thrown two of his victims into the Green River. At least, all they'd found so far. They suspected he was also responsible for a few other missing girls in the area. I stood up and walked closer to the screen so I could hear the reporter better.

"A woman who was attacked said she met her assailant at a restaurant in Snoqualmie. They walked to her car, and once they reached it he leaned down and started to strangle her. A witness to the incident was walking by and saw a man towering over a woman with his hands around her throat."

Stuff like that just doesn't happen around here. Maybe in Spokane, but not here. We do get some tourists, since that show *Twin Peaks* was filmed around here. I think they used that diner in North Bend, and the hotel in Snoqualmie. I watched an episode once with Dev. It was a weird show, but maybe I just didn't get it.

I sat down and waited. I didn't see a lot of hospital workers, or cops. It didn't feel right. I know this is a small town, but a lot happened tonight. The high school quarterback was brought in on a stretcher. They haven't even told us what's wrong with him yet. And the Green River Copycat Killer is here, why isn't this place filled with cops?

Sheriff Monet walked into the waiting room. I walked up to her.

"Hi, Sheriff Monet."

"Hello. Drew, right?"

"That's right! I was wondering what was going on. I mean, I know you guys have that serial killer here."

"Yes, but don't worry. The FBI is on their way, and he'll be under their custody soon."

Not much else they can do until the FBI takes over I guess. I looked at Cerie. She was still talking to Joey. She glanced away from him. Was she looking for me?

"Drew!" I heard someone call my name. It sounded like Mom. I turned around.

"I just heard from the nurse that they have to transfer your brother to the hospital in Seattle. He has a concussion, and they saw some bleeding in his brain."

I nodded and Mom patted my arm. She said she was still having trouble getting Dad on the phone. He didn't even know what was going on.

There wasn't much else we could do but wait for the ambulance to come pick up Dev. Mom went to look at the magazine rack. I sat down going back and forth from watching the TV to Cerie.

My mind kept wandering to Dev. Suddenly my past with him was all I could see and it scared me, like he was going to die and I was seeing our life flash before my eyes.

We have one of those relationships that I wonder if other siblings have, where we compete with each other, but also can't live without each other.

I love my brother, but there've been times when he's bugged me. He always gets the girls. Every time we go out, to the movies, or to a game, the girls are all over him. It's like they see him first, and won't even give me a second glance.

He's more popular with the teachers, too. He picked up the alphabet quicker, he learned how to read sooner. Not so much because he was a grade ahead of me, but the time it took him to learn everything was quicker than it took me.

My learning skills were always compared to Dev. My third grade teacher said on the first day that Devin Mathers had been the perfect straight-A student, and that she hoped I would live up to him.

Do you know what it's like to live like that? Constantly being reminded that someone who looks a lot like you had already been there and done that. It's really annoying. It's almost like being a younger sibling means you can't be yourself. You're an extension of your older sibling. I always hated that.

When I got to high school he always sat with me at lunch. Everyone likes Dev, so they're cool with me. When they see me alone in the hallway they'll say "Hey!" but they never chat or hang out with me, unless they're looking for Dev. They'll ask if I'd seen Dev, thank me and then leave. That's about it.

But when it's just me and Dev hanging out together, no girls, no kids from school, I like that. We have a connection that I know he doesn't have with anyone else. He's different when we're alone. When we're at school, he has a smile plastered on his face the whole time. I think that's why everyone likes him, he always looks happy. But at the end of the day, the smile usually goes away and he looks more relaxed.

Lightning struck outside, the whole waiting room lit up. Then rain pounded against the windows. The football players and the cheerleaders wandered into the waiting room and took up the middle seats, the same way they did in the cafeteria at school.

There was a rumble of thunder and a couple of the cheerleaders jumped. I looked over at Cerie, she seemed calm. Another reason I liked her.

She looked up and right into my eyes. It was obvious I'd been staring at her so I turned my head to the TV. They were still talking about the copycat killer.

"Another victim was found near Spokane. She was in her early twenties, and is currently unidentified. Her hands had been chopped off…"

There was another big rumble of thunder and a bright streak of lightning. The lights went out and then I heard this loud whir. The backup generator must've kicked in, because in a split second the lights were back on. But that didn't stop some people from freaking out, like the two little kids with their aunt, not to mention a couple of the cheerleaders.

"What's going on?" I asked Sheriff Monet.

"Stay calm, probably just from the storm. I'm going to check in with the deputy guarding the room."

I noticed she unclipped her side holster as she walked away. That made me a little nervous. I looked around for Mom, and then Cerie. They were sitting somewhat near each other. I walked over.

"You guys alright?"

They both nodded and then I heard feet pounding against the linoleum. Someone was running down the hallway.

"I've got an officer down, I need backup!"

Waiting Room

Sheriff Monet ran past the waiting room shouting into her walkie-talkie. She called out for Nurse Tracey.

"What's going on?" Mom stood up.

"I don't know, it doesn't sound good." I walked over to the doorway. I didn't see anyone so I stepped out. It's a pretty small hospital, so I figured I should see someone who worked there soon enough. I walked around the hall to the main desk. It was empty. Then I heard feet pounding on the floor again. More than just one set of them.

Coming around the bend of the big U that made the hospital was Nurse Tracey, the guy in scrubs who'd wheeled Dev away, and Sheriff Monet tailing them.

"Move it!" She called out. I didn't know if she was talking to me or the other two, but they were heading straight for me anyway so I decided to run with them. We all ran into the waiting room. Sheriff Monet stopped at the door and stood there with her gun in her hands.

"Everyone remain calm. We're waiting for backup. We had a suspect in custody who has escaped. He's most likely left the premises by now, but to be on the safe side everyone needs to stay in the waiting room for now."

"What about the patients?" Nurse Tracey said.

"Yes, my son is here!" Mom spoke up.

"So is my sister!" The aunt with the two kids said, and drew the girls in closer to her.

"We'll stand guard by their rooms."

"Who is 'we'? The other cop is dead, there's just you now!" The guy in scrubs spoke up. I didn't know if he was a nurse or a doctor.

"Backup is on the way. The FBI should be here any minute."

"But what about the roads?" Mrs. Cooper said from behind me. I hadn't noticed she was still here.

"What about them?" Sheriff Monet said.

"On the news, they were talking about a number of downed trees in the area. Some of the roads are blocked right now."

Sheriff Monet didn't say "Dammit!" but I swear her mouth moved with the words.

"Can I help?" I raised my hand like I was in class.

"Andrew!" Mom tugged at my hand, and she said my full name which she almost never did.

"How do you feel about standing guard at the patient rooms?" Sheriff Monet said.

"I'll stand by Dev's room!" I looked over at Dev's friends. The cheerleaders were looking at me with big round eyes. It was nice. A couple of the guys actually looked pissed at me. Maybe they were mad they hadn't thought of it. One of them stood up. Joey Venereaux, that jerk.

"I'll stand guard too." He raised his hand. A couple of the cheerleaders now looked at him with big eyes.

"Okay great," Mom said and clapped me on the back. "He'll stand guard for you. Drew, sit down."

"Mom…" I rolled my eyes at her.

"Actually we need all the bodies we can get," Sheriff Monet said. "How many patients are there?"

"Four." Nurse Tracey said. "Well, three now. The fourth was the guy who escaped."

"And Dr. Pulaski is in his office," the other person in scrubs said. "That's the whole staff here for the overnight shift, just us nurses and the attending doctor."

So I found out he's a nurse, now I had to find out what his name is.

"You." Sheriff Monet pointed at me. "And you." She pointed at Joey. "Come with us."

Waiting Room

We followed her and the nurses into the hallway. Sheriff Monet turned around to look at us. She walked backward.

"This is Nurse Tracey, and Nurse Henry." She looked at me. "Drew, right?"

"That's right. I'm Drew Mathers, Devin's brother."

"I didn't catch your name." She looked at Joey.

"Joey Venereaux, fullback."

Why did he have to say he was the fullback? Man, I hate this guy.

"Alright. Nurses, let us know what rooms the patients are in."

"Mr. McAllister is over here," Henry pointed to the room closest to the waiting room. "He came in complaining of chest pains. He's ninety-one, but seems like he's doing okay. He's resting right now."

"Over here is Ginger Loring," Tracey said. "Her kids are the ones in the waiting room with her sister. She came in with abdominal pain, suspected food poisoning."

"Then we have the star quarterback Devin Mathers." Henry winked at me.

"Do you think he'll be okay?" I asked.

"His leg is broken and we had to put in a transfer call to bring him to Seattle. He's got a concussion and the CT scan showed a small amount of bleeding."

"We're a really small hospital," Tracey said. "We transfer a lot of patients to Seattle."

I must have looked upset, because Tracey asked if I was okay, then nudged Henry.

"I'm fine. Can I go in to see Dev?"

"Sure." Tracey led me into the room.

She pulled back the curtain and I looked at Dev laid out on the hospital bed. They had the bottom part raised up so his leg was elevated. He'd really busted it. He'll probably be on crutches for a while, miss this season.

"He's going to be okay, right?" I looked at Tracey.

"In my experience, people with concussions usually are."

Usually? That didn't make me feel much better, but it's not like she can promise me he'll be okay. She's not the doctor who'll be treating him. Even they can't make that promise.

I stood by his door and Sheriff Monet gave me her nightstick for a weapon. She had Joey stand near Ginger Loring's room, and gave him a walkie-talkie to call her on if he saw anything. I didn't think that was much of a weapon.

Sheriff Monet said she would stand guard between the door to the waiting room and the older guy's room, the one with the chest pain. I already forgot his name. She assured all of us that the hospital was small enough, she could get to us in time if we needed her.

Tracey went to get the doctor. I watched her walk a few doors down from where I stood outside Dev's room, and when she opened the door to the doctor's office she screamed. Sheriff Monet came running over.

"Dr. Pulaski's dead!" Tracey said through tears. Sheriff Monet ushered her into the doctor's office.

I took a few steps toward them, and then the door to my left opened. Slowly. I tiptoed backward into Dev's room and eased against the wall. I peered out, and watched a man with a limp wearing a hospital gown creep down the hall, a bloody scalpel in his hand.

I looked at Dev. His eyes were closed. I took a deep breath and then stepped out of his room. Being as quiet as I could, I held onto the nightstick and followed the man with the scalpel.

Waiting Room

His limp was so much like Dad's it was freaky. His build was the same, and he had the same hair, brown and shaggy in the back. As I walked behind him I was almost convinced that if he turned around I would see my father's face.

I thought about the hand at the beach last summer and the news reports I'd heard that night. The woman found near Spokane. How Mom couldn't reach Dad on his cell. All night.

I swallowed. My neck was wet with sweat. The guy with the scalpel moved so slowly he was like the killer from the old *Halloween* movies.

He walked toward the waiting room. I didn't know what to do. Should I yell out to Sheriff Monet? Or would that make him turn around and attack me? Would that scalpel cut through the nightstick like a Ginsu knife?

He started picking up the pace so I did too. He was almost around the corner, and in sight of the door to the waiting room. I didn't know what he was planning to do, and I didn't see Sheriff Monet anywhere.

Without thinking much about it, I ran up behind him wielding the nightstick. Someone must have seen him because there was a scream. The guy with the scalpel turned around.

I brought the nightstick down onto his head as he was turning. He stumbled backward and then he charged at me. The next thing I saw was his body convulse as the bullet Sheriff Monet fired went through him.

The entire time I never looked at his face. I was too afraid to. But I made myself look when he was down on the ground.

The Green River Copycat Killer, though he resembled my father from behind, wasn't him. He had scars on his cheeks, a crooked nose and an earring. His face didn't resemble my father's at all.

"Are you alright?" Sheriff Monet trotted toward me and lowered her gun. I nodded at her. She went into the waiting room and calmed everyone down. Mom was calling my name.

"Drew, thank God you're okay. What are you doing with that?"

She pointed at the nightstick I was still holding. I pointed at the guy on the floor, and mimicked hitting him over the head with it.

"That was a very dangerous thing to do!"

I looked around, hoping Cerie was nearby to hear that. She wasn't, of course.

"I heard from your father, by the way."

"Oh, you did?"

"The reception in this part of town is awful. He apparently left me a message a while ago that only just showed up in my phone."

"What did he say?"

"He'd heard about what happened to your brother, one of his coworkers knew someone at the game and told him so he was already on his way here. He should be here any minute."

Suddenly lights were flashing everywhere.

"The ambulance is here for the transfer," Henry said and went to the main doors.

The paramedics were wheeling in a stretcher with someone strapped to it, not an empty stretcher to pick someone up.

"What happened?" Henry asked them as he bent down closer to the guy on the stretcher.

Waiting Room

"We were on our way here and some of the roads were blocked. Flooding, downed power lines, we heard it over the scanner. Then we got a call about a car wreck not far from here. Some guy skid into a tree, car totaled."

"Jeez, he doesn't look good." Henry peered into the guy's face with his penlight. That was when I saw who the guy was.

"Dad?" I ran over. Mom followed me.

"Oh my God! Is he okay?"

Henry held out his hands to us, in a "back off" gesture.

"Please step back," he said. "We have to transfer him to Seattle as well."

"You can't be serious!" Mom screamed. I put my arm around her.

"Ma'am, our attending physician was murdered tonight! We don't have anyone here who can treat him."

"What kind of hospital is this?"

"Mom, please calm down."

Dad started shaking all over. Henry wheeled him into one of the rooms. I brought Mom to the waiting room. Cerie saw us and came over, I told her what happened. She held Mom's hand, and came with us to Seattle. We followed the two ambulances.

We found out when we got there that Dad didn't make the trip. He died on the way to the other hospital. Mom screamed at the paramedics but the doctor assured her there was nothing they could've done. Something about internal bleeding.

I held my mother as she cried. I wanted to cry too, but I wanted to be strong for her. Sometimes being strong for someone else keeps you from feeling sad, at least for the time being. I held it back, and felt my body grow numb inside.

It lasted until the day of the funeral. After we got back and everyone left, and it was just me and Mom and Dev in the house, no Dad, I lost it. I was in my room and found one of his hiking photos in the desk drawer. He always took a shot of the sunset. I cried with it in my hands as I fell asleep.

The good news was that Dev was okay. I know that this is one of those horrible things I'm not supposed to say, I'm not even supposed to think it, but I'm so glad Dev made it. If I had to pick between him or Dad, I can survive without my dad. I can't live without my brother.

Dev was out for the season, and took to writing short stories. He really likes it, said he's thinking about not playing ball next year after his leg heals. He wants to take creative writing classes, and he's been just as popular off the field. The kids at school actually started hanging around me as much as Dev, but I didn't care about it so much.

Cerie and I have been dating. Pretty seriously, too. There's something about being in a situation like we were in that gives you this automatic closeness. We even talked about going to the same college after graduation.

Mom really misses Dad. She had to go back to work, but she seems to like it, said it keeps her busy. I miss Dad too, and wish he could've seen me with Cerie. I know he would've given me a pat on the back and said "Nice job, kiddo." I also wish he could've seen me clonk a crazy serial killer's head with a nightstick. He would've patted me on the back for that too.

I never told anyone how I'd suspected Dad had been the killer, even for a second. At least Dad didn't die knowing that. That's all that matters. I'll never tell anyone about that one. That's guilt I'll have to live with all by myself, but I'm okay with it. I really am. I keep waiting and waiting for that guilty feeling to go away, but it hasn't yet. But I'm okay with that. I really am. As long as I keep telling myself I'm okay, that makes it true, right?

Jenna Moquin

The Reward Program

Cornered in the alley, Jones stood in a triangle with Davies and McMurphy, their backs against each other. In the crowd that surrounded them, Jones could make out very few faces. The alley was dark and the streetlamps on the main road were too dim to reach beyond a few feet.

The crowd of men held an array of wooden objects: long, thick tree branches, baseball bats, and many two-by-four jagged boards, some with nails sticking out of them. Jones then realized that the action of Martial Law that took away firearms from civilians didn't do anything to quell the use of weapons.

He looked through the crowd again as his eyes refocused in the darkness, and three familiar faces appeared amidst the menacing pieces of wood.

"That's Sully!" Jones whispered. Sully had worked in the cubicle next to him at Gordon Supply in lower Manhattan, what felt like centuries ago. He nudged Davies, and nodded toward Sully. Davies nudged McMurphy, who shook his head.

"And there's Remy and Kohl." Jones looked a few feet away from Sully, and saw two more former cubicle mates.

"Why are they doing this?" McMurphy said.

"You know why." Davies tapped the plastic badge on McMurphy's lapel. The badge was painted gold, and resembled a child's police badge, the kind that came with plastic handcuffs and a toy gun. Written across the badge in black letters were the words "Reward Program Deputy."

The Reward Program began soon after Martial Law was declared in 2049. After an economic collapse that caused civil war within the United States, the military and police were understaffed, overworked and enlisted the help of average citizens.

The program offered rewards such as food, money, and clothing to those who signed up, and the deputies reported to the police and government offices whenever they observed criminal behavior in their neighborhood.

"Look guys," Jones said. He lifted his shaking palms and raised his voice to the crowd. "We don't want any trouble. Just let us go, alright? We were only trying to get by, same as the rest of you!"

Sully guffawed and spat on the pavement.

"It's true!" Jones dropped his hands. "We all lost our jobs, and the whole damn country is in the worst mess we've ever been in. We're all scared, we're all desperate for survival."

"We're all scared." Remy's southern accent rose out of the crowd. "You're right. But not all of us would stoop to what you three are doing!"

"Hey!" McMurphy stared at Remy. "If those people were following the laws, they wouldn't be in jail now."

Laughter rippled throughout the crowd and Sully held up a hand to quiet them.

"That's the oldest excuse," Sully said. "Isn't it? 'If they were just following the law...' The laws are wrong, McMurphy."

"Good ole George Orwell had it right." Kohl spoke for the first time, and lowered his wooden board. "He just had the wrong year."

After the Global Wars, a new version of the Constitution of the United States was created. It was signed by the President and passed in the House of Representatives in 2042, and called The Citizens Constitution. Some viewed it to be a glorified version of the first Patriot Act, and soon the original Constitution along with the Declaration of Independence was banned.

The new laws enforced body scanners at not just airport terminals but train stations, malls, even schools. Every citizen was implanted with microchips that held all of their personal information such as medical history and banking records.

"I can't even buy bread at the store without getting a retinal scan," Kohl said. "And I used to think it was silly to give an I.D. to buy cough syrup!"

"Ain't that the truth," Sully said. "America used to be the land of the free. Now they got people spying on each other with this damn Reward Program."

Jones, Davies and McMurphy huddled closer against each other. Davies was farthest from the crowd, and slyly removed a cigarette from his pocket and lit it. He was thinking about his wife who was waiting for him at home. She said they were having a pot roast for dinner.

McMurphy's mind was on the whereabouts of his brother, another Reward Program Deputy. He was currently patrolling a street two blocks away. He prayed that his brother wouldn't come near this alley.

Jones thought about his wife and little girl, and felt grateful that they were visiting friends in New Jersey. He didn't want them to see what he would look like after an ambush beating by a group of angry men. He couldn't believe it had come to something like this. He wanted to try and talk some sense into his former co-workers.

"Sully, you have to understand! I couldn't find a job, I had to feed and clothe my family!" Jones tried to look into his eyes. "I'm actually surprised none of you signed up to be deputies!"

"Don't you get it?" Remy shook his head. "They destroyed our country, took away everything that made us free."

"Who is 'they' Remy?" Jones shook his head. "The economy fell, it just happened. It's no one's fault!"

"No, it didn't just happen. It was planned for years to create the world we all live in now. And the 'they' I'm referring to, well you know damn well who it is. We used to talk about this in the office, remember? You thought I was joking, said I was crazy."

Remy pointed up to a spot behind Jones' head. He gazed up and saw one of the many billboards that were scattered throughout New York and the rest of the country.

A shining white backdrop framed an outline of a black heart. Inside the heart was six words: I Love the New World Order.

"So a new world order came out of the mess we got ourselves into. What else was the government supposed to do?" Jones shouted. His pulse was racing.

"The government!" Remy's voice rose. "They were behind the economy falling!"

"Them among others," Kohl added.

"These guys are crazy!" McMurphy sounded close to tears.

"We're crazy, huh?" Sully spat on the ground. "Crazy for fighting to take back our country? And you, Jones. You always thought you were better than me."

"I am better than you," Jones said. "I'm not the one cornering my former colleagues and threatening them."

"No, you're just sending them to jail for – what was Collier arrested for again?" Sully turned toward Remy.

"For putting up posters with quotes from The Constitution. You know, the real one written in the 1700s."

"That's right." Sully nodded. "You ratted out Collier to those Martial Law freaks. The next day they broke down his door, used a Taser on him in front of his wife and kids, and hauled him off to another country where he's probably being water-boarded. All because the government declared him a 'terrorist.' For putting up the words of our founding fathers. It makes me sick!"

"But it's against the law to post any document that's been banned by the government," Jones said as he cowered near Davies and McMurphy. "It's a Level Three Offense!"

"So you're okay with them banning books, forcing us to be microchipped and walk through scanners, and making us all live like rats in a cage?"

"I never said I was okay with it. I'm following the law, just trying to get by."

"I bet a lot of those Nazis in Germany said that too when they herded up their neighbors and put them into camps." Sully tapped his board against his palm.

"You really should let us go," Jones said. "We won't report you to anyone. But if you hurt us, you're opening the door to prison for yourselves."

"Yeah, let 'em try and catch all of us!" Sully laughed, and with a swift gesture of his hand, the entire crowd swarmed around Jones, Davies, and McMurphy.

Sully struck Jones in his shoulder with the wooden board. Jones shut his eyes and covered his face with his hands. He didn't bother to see how Davies and McMurphy were faring.

Then Sully's board met the back of Jones's head, and as he blacked out he heard the sound of a helicopter above. In seconds, the helicopter hovered over the crowd in the alley, and soon shots were fired from it. Remy looked up, punched McMurphy and then bolted down the alley. Bullets chased after him, but he disappeared into a dark corner.

McMurphy waved his arms at the helicopter, and pointed to the badge on his lapel.

"I'm with you guys! I'm with you!" He shouted before bullets pelted into his chest.

A steady stream of gunfire came out of the sky and shot into the rest of the crowd, and when there was no longer any movement in the alley, the helicopter left.

Remy waited until the helicopter was gone and tiptoed back to the alley. He found Sully's body, grasped the chain around his neck and yanked it off. Hanging from the bloodied chain was a locket that Remy snapped open. Inside was a tiny photo of Sully's daughter.

Remy stuffed it into his pocket and closed Sully's eyelids with his thumb and forefinger. He left the alley just as two large vans turned the corner.

He remained out of sight while he watched the clean-up crew remove the bodies, and when he saw Sully's body carried out he bowed his head.

"They won't get us all," Remy whispered.

On Remy's walk back to his apartment, he passed a young man wearing a Reward Program Deputy badge on his lapel.

"Evenin' sir," Remy said and nodded at the man.

The deputy nodded back, and hung his head as he passed. Remy wondered if Jones was right, that the deputies in the program were just as scared as everyone else in the new world. Remy heard helicopters nearby and quickened his pace, keeping his head down. He wasn't sure what else to do besides continue walking forward with his head down, and the deputy did the same.

Things That Go Bump in the Morning

With a yawn Melanie started to wake up. She'd been dreaming about her honeymoon in La Jolla. She was on the beach and the sun streamed onto her back, warm and inviting. When she realized it was the sun seeping in through the blinds she woke up completely, and yawned again with a stretch. That was when she felt something small and furry moving up her spine.

"There's something on my back!" She shouted. "Get it off! What is it?"

"Mel," Glen said as he got out of bed. "There's nothing there."

His wife had vivid dreams, and sometimes talked in her sleep. One time she was dreaming about falling off a cliff, and woke up screaming as she fell to the floor, and bumped her head.

"I can feel it, something is crawling on me! Is it a mouse?"

When they first moved into The Belmont, Glen found a mouse in the kitchen. They hadn't seen another since they had the exterminator over, but Melanie was still worried about them. She wanted to move as soon as their lease was up.

"Baby," Glen said. "I think you're still dreaming, because there's nothing on your back."

"Okay."

Melanie sniffed and pushed herself up with her elbows. As soon as she did she screamed, and that's when Glen did see something on her back, small drops of blood.

"What the...?"

He reached down to check the wounds, and his hand took hold of something furry with lots of tentacles. It writhed in his grip, but he saw nothing in his hand. He felt a sharp pain, and blood oozed out of tiny marks on his finger. He threw the invisible creature against the wall and heard a soft thud.

"What is it?" Melanie grabbed a t-shirt and pressed it against her back.

For once he didn't have an answer for her. Usually he was Mr. Fix-It, with everything from a broken taillight to a computer crash, he had an explanation and solution for every problem. Glen stared at his wife with a look she'd never seen before.

"It's on me!" Melanie shook her leg as drops of blood appeared on her ankle. Glen reached down and grabbed the creature. He held it while he tried to figure out where its teeth were.

He found them when another sharp pain stung his hand, and he slammed the creature into the wall above the laundry basket. His hand was roughly four inches away from the wall.

He tried to ignore the squeamish feeling in his stomach as it writhed in his hand and its tentacles wrapped themselves around his fingers.

Melanie pulled on a large parka from the closet, and then a pair of ski pants. She found Glen's ski clothes behind his trench coat, and carried them over to him.

"Thanks, but I'm afraid to let go of this thing."

"At least you can put on the pants, they'll help block its teeth."

Melanie helped him shimmy into the ski pants. There was still a tear in the seam from their trip to Nashoba Valley last winter that she kept forgetting to mend.

"What are we going to do? And why can't we see it?"

"I'm going to kill it, like I would any other pest." He didn't bother trying to guess her second question. He focused on the one solution he had.

"Bring me a large screwdriver," Glen said. "Or a butcher knife."

Melanie scurried out of the bedroom, happy to have a chore to focus on as she tried not to think too much about what this creature was, and why they couldn't see it. She hoped she was still dreaming, because her mind couldn't get around it. She ransacked the kitchen drawers until she found a knife and rushed back to the bedroom.

"Hurry up! I can't hold this thing much longer."

Melanie handed him the knife.

"Glen, why can't we see it?"

"We'll worry about that later. Let's just get rid of it."

He steadied his grip on the creature, and held the knife with the blade pointed toward the wall. He breathed through his nose and relaxed his shoulders.

Glen held the knife, and stabbed it through the creature and into the wall. He felt around the blade, and there was fur attached to a slack mass.

A gelatinous liquid he couldn't see oozed through his fingers, and Glen felt satisfied that it was dead. He wiped his hands on a towel and went over to Melanie.

"Baby, it's over. I killed it."

She looked up to where he pointed at the wall, and saw nothing but the knife sticking out.

"You killed it, Glen?"

"Yeah, now what do we do with it?"

"I think we should see a doctor about these bites."

Glen couldn't decide if he should call animal control or NASA. It was invisible, but they could feel it, especially when it bit them. Their wounds were proof.

But when he glanced down at his hand he didn't see anything. No blood, no bite marks, nothing. He asked Melanie to remove her parka so he could check her back, and those wounds were gone as well.

"What's wrong? Are the bites worse?"

"Um, no. They're just gone...do yours still hurt?"

"No, actually."

Melanie was surprised to realize that she hadn't felt any pain in a while. She'd been too preoccupied to notice. Her eyes widened as she looked at the knife in the wall.

"Was that real? Did it really happen?"

Glen walked over to the knife and touched the area around it, and felt nothing but cracked plaster.

"I don't believe it!"

"What's wrong?"

"There's nothing there. Just the knife. But I felt this stuff ooze out of it. Did it disintegrate when I stabbed it? Turn into dust like a vampire?"

Glen chuckled, but he didn't feel very humorous.

Melanie stared at the wall, and wondered if it was all a dream, the most horribly vivid dream she'd ever had. Maybe any moment she'd wake up to Glen snuggling against her back asking if she was in the mood before coffee that morning.

She closed her eyes and urged herself to wake up. She told herself that when she opened them, she'd be back in bed beside her husband. But when she opened her eyes,

Things That Go Bump in the Morning

Glen was still staring at the wall as if it held all the answers to what had happened to them that morning.

Melanie sighed and looked down, and saw a small bump in the carpet that crept toward her.

"Glen, I think that's it!" She pointed at the bump, whose movement quickened.

"Is that the same one, or are there more of them?" Glen shouted.

He rushed over and stomped on it with his foot, but it moved too fast and he missed it by an inch. He stomped again, but it disappeared. He felt like he was playing Whack-A-Mole at the carnival. Melanie picked up a hardcover book and threw it on the bump.

"Did I get it?"

They both scanned the floor, looking for movement. Glen picked up the book and peered at the carpet. He pressed down, but didn't feel anything. Melanie looked up and saw movement out of the corner of her eye.

"There!" She pointed.

A bump was near the door where the bedroom carpet ended. The bump vanished, and through the open door, Melanie saw the bump reappear in the hallway carpet heading toward the kitchen. She ran after it trying to stomp it, but it kept dodging her feet.

Glen ran ahead of her into the kitchen and grabbed a knife. He stood with his feet planted on the linoleum and waited at the entrance of the kitchen where the hallway carpet ended. He watched the bump move to the edge of the carpet.

The carpet inched upward and then fell flat, and he stabbed the floor next to it. He kept stabbing the knife around the same radius of a few inches and scratched the floor in several places before he gave up. Panting and sweating, he looked at Melanie, who had grabbed a knife of her own.

"I haven't seen the bump again, I think you got it!" She said with a smile.

"Yeah, well, I thought I got it before so I'm not getting my hopes up."

"Come here."

Melanie reached out with her free hand and stroked Glen's back. He leaned down and nestled his nose in her neck, and breathed that scent he loved.

In the mornings she wafted this mixture of wet roses and baby powder, he'd always found it intoxicating. She kissed his chin, and he kissed her lips. He wanted to pick her up and carry her to the bedroom, and try to pretend the morning had just begun when her back arched and she gasped in pain.

Glen swiveled her around and saw blood on her lower back. He reached down and caught the creature in his hand.

He threw it to the floor and grasped it while he jabbed the knife through. Again he felt thick liquid ooze out, but he didn't let go. After a few seconds, he didn't feel anything at all.

The creature had disappeared, and with a groan Glen stabbed the floor. It was infuriating trying to find something he couldn't see, and he didn't want to wait for one of them to get bitten again to find it.

If there was an infestation of invisible creatures, he wasn't quite sure how to explain these pests to the exterminator. And if it was the same creature continually coming back to life, that was even scarier.

"There!" Melanie pointed with the knife at the hallway carpet, where another bump had appeared.

She chased it down the hallway and stabbed at it but kept missing. She didn't even care about all the repairs they'd have to do in the coming weeks. She just wanted all of this to be over.

Glen ran ahead to the carpet's edge by the bedroom door. He crouched and held the knife. When the bump in the carpet got closer, he brought the knife down and stabbed the floor. He touched around the tip of the knife with his fingers, but didn't feel anything. Then he felt it on his chest, crawling upward.

"It's on me!"

"I can't stab you!" Melanie said with a pout. Glen grabbed the creature from his chest and didn't even wince when it bit his palm.

"Let's try to burn it this time. Go turn on the oven."

Before they could try their new plan, Glen felt the creature disappear from his hand. He didn't know if it fell to the floor, flew away or if it could teleport.

The fact that they couldn't see it was making him lean toward teleporting, but that was something that happened in sci-fi movies, not real life. The sort of thing he'd see on the old *Twilight Zone* shows he used to watch with his dad. Glen cursed and kicked the dresser, then cursed again at his stubbed toe.

Melanie screamed and fell to the floor. Blood appeared in tiny drops all over her. She screamed and squirmed and Glen, who didn't normally cry, began to sob.

Through the blur of his tears, he saw something on Melanie's torso. It had silver fur and a dozen tentacles and beady red eyes. It looked like a cross between a spider and a bat, and just as creepy as something like that would look.

He could finally see the creature, and see where its head was. He gripped the knife and brought it down, but the second the tip of the knife grazed its fur it disappeared again, and the knife went into Melanie's chest.

Blood poured out and her eyes widened as she looked at Glen, who stared at her with tears streaming down his face.

"What…what did I…?"

He stammered and reached for the handle of the knife.

"Don't!" Melanie's voice was growing hoarse. "Don't take it out. Call 911!"

Glen started to rise when the creature crawled up his leg and bit him all over. He fell to his knees beside her, swatting at the creature.

Melanie saw drops of blood appear on his stomach and chest, and then she saw a silvery flash. She blinked and looked again, and saw the creature crawling up Glen's shoulder. She watched it bite into his neck so deeply blood spurted out, causing him to fall over.

Melanie didn't realize she was still holding up her own knife. When Glen fell, it went into his stomach.

She stared into his eyes, and he stared back at her, looking so frightened she just wanted to comfort him. A bloody cough was all that came out when she tried to tell Glen she loved him.

She reached out and took his hand and squeezed it, faintly. He squeezed back and they closed their eyes as the blood pooled around them. Soon the world around them swam into blurred shapes and colors, and then pure darkness.

Three days later, the superintendent unlocked the door to number twenty-two at The Belmont, with Melanie's sister behind him. The scent inside the apartment swarmed at them, as if it had been waiting for that door to open just so it could run out and let loose in the hallway.

Things That Go Bump in the Morning

They covered their noses and coughed before they walked inside. A couple of flies were swatted at, and they headed toward the bedroom at the end of the hall, where the smell was strongest.

The superintendent eased the door open, and dozens of flies buzzed around the room.

On the floor were the bodies of Glen and Melanie Wapenski. Melanie had a knife sticking out of her chest, Glen beside her with a knife in his stomach. A larger knife was stuck inside the wall above the laundry basket.

Melanie's sister screamed. She fell to her knees, wailing. One of the flies flew into her mouth, and then flew out. Then she ran into the bathroom and vomited. The superintendent left to call the medical examiner, and to find a can of bug spray.

The police arrived later, and after searching they seemed confident it was a simultaneous homicide, or a murder-suicide, no matter how much Melanie's sister insisted they were a happy couple.

She was convinced someone had broken in and killed them, even though there wasn't any evidence of a break-in and nothing appeared stolen.

The scratches on the floor and tears in the carpet only seemed to back up the detective's theory that a violent fight had taken place before they killed each other.

Several other residents in the building had gathered around apartment twenty-two to see what was going on, and what the smell had been.

A small bump appeared in the hallway carpet leading to the stairs, but nobody noticed through all of the commotion.

Jenna Moquin

The bump in the carpet reached the entrance door to The Belmont, and then disappeared. Later that morning, in an apartment two blocks away, a woman screamed.

Indictment

I stared at the paper inside Nelson's briefcase. It was a flight confirmation printout, one seat on a one-way flight to Bali. We were supposed to go to Bali for our next vacation. We, not one.

I thought back to our honeymoon in Florida, how we'd made love twice a day. But we never had sex again during a trip. Usually we spent vacations fighting. For some reason, Nelson seemed to be more stressed out during vacations than he was at work.

When we moved into separate bedrooms a few years back, I didn't think much of it. We were so thrilled over getting a bigger house with more rooms, and each of us having our own suite made us feel like the king and queen of the castle. I loved the sprawling backyard, even though it was mostly desert with a view of Vegas in the background, and Nelson loved the two-car garage. He purchased a BMW not long after that, and we were in heaven.

But then it came out exactly how Nelson got all of that money. The newspapers revealed he was embezzling funds along with three others at the investment company. They said he'd been doing it for years. I was shocked.

What hurts the most was how he'd kept it hidden from me, all this time. I heard about his arrest by reading it in the newspaper. He told me he was on a business trip to Manhattan when he called me from jail.

We used to be each other's best friend. Neither of us had siblings, and we both came from small families. It was one of the things that I always thought connected us. After the move into separate bedrooms, I started to feel a shift in the connection. He seemed less interested in how I spent my days while he spent more and more time at the office. But I never said anything about it. Perhaps I didn't want to admit that something was wrong. Does anyone ever want to admit that?

As I held his flight confirmation, a tear fell and hit the paper. Then Nelson walked in. I didn't even hear him come up the stairs.

"Laney, what are you doing?"

"What am I doing? What the hell are you doing?"

"You really shouldn't have looked in there."

I threw the piece of paper at him. It fluttered to the carpet.

"You're leaving town? You're under indictment, Nelson!"

He took a few steps closer to me and picked up the ticket to Bali. He was breathing through his nostrils.

"What did you think you were going to do, skip town and become a fugitive? What the hell has gotten into you?"

He stood there and closed his briefcase. I flicked his shoulder, and he didn't even flinch.

"First you embezzled all that money and stupidly got caught, and now you're trying to leave the country?"

The back of his hand hit my cheek so quickly it didn't hurt at first. I cried out of surprise more than pain. He pushed me onto the bed, picked up his bag and turned around.

It wasn't the first time he hit me. He did it once before, on our trip to Virginia Beach. We had a miserable time between the delayed flight, the lost luggage, and I lost my ring down the airplane toilet. I took it off to wash my hands, there was some turbulence and it fell. I tried to shove my hand into the toilet bowl, but it wouldn't fit. The ring was gone.

When we were in our hotel, gratefully wearing fluffy robes and slippers, Nelson started giving me grief about losing my ring. I felt bad enough as it was, and him making me feel guilty was like being kicked when I was already down.

He said I didn't appreciate how hard he worked, and because I didn't work I had no regard for the value of money. His wedding band was on the dresser next to his Rolex. I picked up his ring and threw it into the toilet, and flushed. That move cost me a black eye.

The next day he replaced both of our wedding bands at a nearby jeweler's. He also bought me a new diamond engagement ring, three times the size of my original. He swore he'd never hit me again, and he never laid a hand on me, until now.

I ran after him and jumped onto his back, put my arms around his neck and squeezed. He bent forward and I toppled to the floor where the carpet ends and the hardwood begins. My forehead hit the floor and my shoulder banged against the plant table.

Nelson's feet came toward me, and his leg went back as if to kick me. When his foot came at me I reached out, grabbed it and bit his ankle. He yelped and lost his balance, and in a second he was on the floor next to me.

I started to get up and then he rolled onto my bottom half, trying to pin me down. To my right was the credenza and on the floor next to it was a pile of hardcover books. I've been into Dennis Lehane lately.

I grabbed the top one from the pile and swung it at Nelson's face. It hit his nose and he leaned off me. I pulled myself out from under him and used the credenza to pull myself up. I looked at my husband as he kneeled on the floor and clutched his nose. When he started to get up I ran past him out of the bedroom. My cell phone was on the table in the hall. He caught me before I made it through the door, grabbed my arm and swung me around.

There was a bright light when his fist connected with my face, and it felt like my cheek exploded. My vision was blurred, but I could see Nelson holding the belt from his terrycloth robe. He lurched and tried to toss it around my neck but I ducked out of the way, and tripped over his golf bag. The driver fell out. I grabbed it as I landed on my knees, and when Nelson came at me wielding the noose I smacked the driver into his crotch.

He yelped and fell to his knees. I backed up still holding the driver. My other hand grabbed the crystal vase on the shelf. I dropped the driver and gripped the vase with both hands. While Nelson held his crotch and moaned, I knocked the vase over his head. It didn't break, but it hit him hard enough to make him fall face down on the carpet. He wasn't moving.

I grabbed my cell from the table and flew down the stairs. I didn't look back while I went out through the side door to the garage. It was then I realized there were no car keys in my hand. I didn't want to go back inside, but I needed keys to start the car.

Standing by the door, I peeked through the little window on top. I would've expected Nelson to chase after me, unless he was completely knocked out from the vase. I waited a few more minutes and then went inside.

I tiptoed through the kitchen, but my keys weren't in the apple-shaped dish where they were supposed to be. They weren't on the kitchen table, any of the counters, or anywhere else I looked. Then I heard a noise from upstairs and ran back outside.

I went into the backyard. It's not quite a backyard, even though it's our property, just an expanse of flat desert with an occasional cactus. The lights of Vegas stood out like beacons. Nothing but darkness around for miles, then bright lights flashing hotel names and logos and the sky beam that shines out of The Luxor.

I never liked living so close to Vegas. Nelson had picked out the house specifically for its view of the city. This was my dream house, except for the lights of Vegas in the background.

The desert is always crisp at night, no matter what time of year. I was upset that I didn't grab a sweater or jacket, but even more upset I didn't have car keys. I knelt behind one of the big cacti and called the police from my cell. At least I remembered to grab that on my way out. I wanted to yell at the dispatcher, and see if that would get them to hurry. I spoke in a screaming whisper, my words jumbling into each other.

"Yes, my husband attacked me, how many times do I have to say it? His name is Nelson Cole. That should ring a bell, he's been in all the papers... if you talk to the FBI tell them he's planning on skipping town. Hurry up!"

I chewed on my lip as I waited. For the first time in four years I desperately wanted a cigarette. I kept my eyes on the house but our bedroom was on the opposite side so I couldn't see if Nelson was still lying on the carpet, but I didn't see any movement through the other windows.

The cops always take their time around here. I guess they're too busy with the craziness of the city, both downtown and the main strip. Too many drunk tourists acting like it's their last night on earth. I shivered and wrapped my arms around myself and hoped they'd arrive soon.

Twenty minutes went by with no movement in the house, but no cops either. I had grown too cold to stay out there and too curious to wait and see if Nelson was knocked out.

Keeping my eyes on the bay window in the living room, which reveals the bottom of the staircase, I crept closer to the house. When there was movement on the ground a few feet away, something that moved an awful lot like a snake, I ran to the house and went inside. The cops were on their way, and I was sure I could keep Nelson at bay until they arrived. Or at least find a safe place to hide.

The kitchen was empty, as were the living room and dining room. I stood at the bottom of the stairs for a moment. Then I walked up, taking one step at a time. The bedroom door came into view. Open just as I'd left it, and on the carpet was Nelson, still lying there. I jogged up the last few steps and stood in the doorway.

What I'd thought was Nelson was actually just his jacket on top of a pillow. He wasn't unconscious. He wasn't even on the floor.

"Hello, Laney."

He was in front of the mirror holding a gun. I didn't know he owned one, but I'd been learning a lot of new things about my husband lately. He pointed the gun at me and I raised my hands.

"I've been watching you outside, waiting for you to come running back."

I wasn't going to tell him I'd called the cops while I was out there, not with a gun pointed at me.

"You've always been so scared of snakes out there."

"You don't have to do this, Nelson. I'll let you leave, I won't try to stop you."

"I wish you'd never seen that ticket to Bali. I would've been on my way right now."

"But I won't say anything, I swear! When the FBI comes to question me I'll tell them I came home tonight and you were gone. I have no idea where you went!"

"I really can't rely on that."

He cocked back the gun, and I ducked just in time to feel the force of a bullet fly over my head and hit the wall.

I threw myself into the hall and then half ran, half fell down the stairs. I didn't look behind and rushed to the front door, and opened it to see another gun pointed at me.

"Freeze!" The cop holding the gun said.

Nelson fired another shot from behind me. It hit the wall above the front door. He apparently hadn't noticed that I'd opened the door to a cop holding a gun. He looked so surprised when the cop fired a round back at him.

The bullet hit Nelson in the middle of his chest. He fell to the floor and got blood on the carpet. All of my bones turned into jelly as I dropped into a heap in the foyer. I barely felt the cop pat my shoulder, and couldn't hear what he was asking me since my ears were ringing. His voice sounded like it was coming from far away. Only two words came through clearly.

"…your husband…"

"That wasn't the man I married." My voice was getting hoarse.

He called for an ambulance, and I tried not to look at Nelson. The cop said I should get some air, and he went over to Nelson on the carpet. The sounds of the gunshots created this atmosphere around me that was dream-like and staggering, it took me a while to stand up and walk a few steps. I went outside. I still didn't have a jacket, but I felt so cold all over it didn't seem like a jacket would do much anyway.

When the paramedics arrived, all they could really do was zip up the body bag. I hung my head as they brought him into the ambulance, and cried. The cop put his arm around me. It all felt so surreal. He wanted to take my statement, and I told him everything that happened that night. My ears were still ringing.

He said they'd be in touch with me, and suggested I contact a lawyer due to Nelson's legal troubles. After he left I went inside, and tried not to look at the bloodstains on the carpet. I went into the kitchen to swallow down the lump in my throat with some wine.

After downing a glass, I looked around at the home that I'd built over the years. The crown moldings I'd picked out, the perfect curtains, the apple-themed kitchen.

It was only a matter of time before the feds would start seizing the assets, including this house. The bank had already frozen his credit cards, something I found out when I tried to buy shoes. I'll be out on the street soon.

I rushed upstairs and looked into Nelson's travel bag. I didn't see any money, no cash or traveler's checks. But I knew about the safe. I only hoped he hadn't made a withdrawal from it already and hid the money somewhere else.

I went into his office and pulled back the desk chair. I crouched down and peeled back a corner of the carpet to reveal the floor safe that Nelson had secretly installed years ago. He always thought he could hide things from me, but he always forgot about my meticulous housecleaning skills.

Luckily the combination was still the date he hit a homerun and won the game for his little league team. Eight-twelve-eighty-eight. It was the same as the code for our alarm system. So easy to remember.

I opened the safe. I smelled the crisp, clean bills before I saw them. There were so many of them, and the increments were in hundreds. I started laughing and crying at the same time.

I closed the safe and put the rug back. When I stood up, my eyes caught the wedding photo on his desk. It was the only picture he liked from our wedding day. We were looking into each other's eyes, not the camera, with these secretive little smiles on our faces. I wanted that moment back so badly.

But then he turned into a different person after we got married. Someone I couldn't trust anymore, someone who hurt me without hesitating. I've heard that happen to a lot of women, almost too many for it to be a coincidence.

I gradually lost my husband over the years. Between the first time he hit me and the separate bedrooms, then the indictment and everything that happened tonight, when I lost him for life. The lump showed up in my throat again, and I sobbed.

I glanced down at the safe. At least he took care of me after he died, that's more than some wives could say. Though I'd trade all of that money to have him back. The man I married, not the man he turned into.

The Dark Gland

Rachel Marx sat on the crisp white sheets that covered her bed. She looked through the window and gazed at the tallest maple tree. A robin flew by and landed on a branch, and she smiled.

Back when she had a job, she'd gaze through the window at the office in between answering calls and filing paperwork. She'd see birds in flight and feel envious of them. They could fly away whenever they pleased, and travel to somewhere they'd never been before. Rachel hadn't felt that envy in a long time.

She sighed and looked around her room at McLean Hospital. It faced east and lost sunlight quickly as the afternoon crept toward evening. There was a strict "Lights Out" call at nine o'clock every night, and she dreaded it every time.

In her lap were a black-and-white speckled notebook and a box of crayons. She pulled out a crayon and turned it over to read the color on the side. Burnt sienna. The color matched her hair, save for the streaks of white at her temples. With another glance through the window, the robin flew away. Rachel opened the notebook and began to write.

* * * * *

The Dark Gland

Dear Dr. Steiner, you wanted this journal since I can't use my voice anymore, and I'll address it to you like I would a diary.

Thanks for the offer of using one of the computers to type this up, but I wanted to do this in the privacy of my room. Besides, I like writing. A pen would be nice, but I understand you guys have rules.

I'll tell you everything that happened, but you must keep your promise that once I hand this in, you'll keep the lights on in my room, all the time.

It started about a year ago. I was having strange dreams and visions at night. The first dream was about a giant-sized little girl dressed in purple playing ball amongst the stars and planets. She walked on the planets like they were stones in a pond, and bounced a red ball against the sun. She laughed in a high-pitched, whirring voice and smiled at me with this big Cheshire cat grin. I saw her every night for a couple of weeks, bouncing that ball, smiling and laughing at me.

Then, as suddenly as she came, I stopped dreaming about her. My office was getting busy and I forgot all about the dreams for a while.

Some nights it took me longer to drift off than usual. Whether it was stress from my job, or fighting with my boyfriend and mother, sometimes thoughts would keep me up and sleep wouldn't come for hours. My eyes would be closed, but I would still be awake.

On those nights when I couldn't fall asleep, I focused on whatever was going on behind my eyelids. It looked like the veins and nerves underneath the skin of my lids. Zigzagging, crisscrossing patterns of bright bluish-white light, sparkles like stars in the sky. Sometimes it felt like I was traveling through outer space, nothing but endless blackness sprinkled with stars.

Later on that same week, the giant little girl in purple showed up. I was in that state between consciousness and unconsciousness right before I drifted off to sleep, and I had a vision of her. She said something that didn't make sense at the time.

"Your pineal gland is a doorway for demons."

Then she morphed into something I've never seen before, a creature that was a cross between a crocodile and a dinosaur, only instead of scales, it had a furry coat like a St. Bernard.

This creature leaped through the stars, jumped over the planets like they were track hurdles. At one point it stopped, turned and stood on its hind legs and looked at me. I don't know if crocodiles can grin, but this creature had the mouth of a crocodile and it grinned at me in the same mischievous way the girl did. Then it pointed at me with a giant claw, and the furry coat disappeared and revealed slimy green scales. It jumped on me and clamped its teeth onto my shoulder and I woke up screaming.

It was so real, I almost expected to see the crocodile creature in my room, smiling at me. My shoulder itched. I went to the bathroom and looked into the mirror. There were marks on my skin where the crocodile bit me in the dream.

I tried to tell myself it was just a dream, and that they were bug bites. A mosquito had found its way inside my room that night and had a feast.

For a while, I didn't have any trouble falling asleep. But that was because I started having a glass or two of wine with dinner, and another glass or two before bedtime. I had uneventful nights, where if I dreamed I didn't remember anything.

Then one night, I had my first vision of the…I don't know what to call it. This creature had the white skull's face of the Grim Reaper with wild frizzy hair. Sort of like a cross between the Grim Reaper and Beetlejuice. The hair color was almost blinding, a fluorescent orange-yellow that waved around its head like fire.

It smiled at me in the same mischievous way as the crocodile, but there was something even worse in that smile, something wretched and sickening. Its eyes shined with a maniacal gleam that swirled with the smile, hypnotizing me. It laughed, the sort of malevolent chortle you'd hear from villains in old movies, and its voice had this strained grating sound like a machine that's breaking down.

It stared at me while it laughed. I opened my eyes to make it go away. I went into the kitchen and drank more wine, since I clearly hadn't had enough to put me to sleep that night.

But after a while, it didn't matter how much I drank, or if I drank at all. That skull's face kept coming back, and sometimes it'd show up when I did nothing but rest my eyes after reading on the sofa.

I never used to believe in the paranormal, ghosts and demons, and things like that. *The Amityville Horror* was just a scary movie, but now I empathize with the people in that family. There are many stories of people saying they were possessed by demons, and I used to think they were crazy. I guess that's what people will say about me.

This skull-face creature haunted me so much I started researching to see if anyone else had a similar experience. There was some comfort in thinking that I might not be alone in this.

I visited message boards and found other people who'd had strange visions, and some even described a Grim Reaper creature. A woman I met online also woke up one morning with a strange rash she couldn't explain, and she described visions of "a vicious man with yellow hair."

I read a lot about dream interpretation. Sigmund Freud believed that dreams were our repressed conscious feelings. Edgar Allen Poe described sleep as "little slices of death." Some theorists have gone the next step, and wondered if we travel somewhere out-of-body when we dream. I'm sure you've heard of astral projection.

One of the books I read was *The Spirit Molecule*. They performed studies on DMT, a psychedelic drug. Some of the people who took it said they traveled to other universes. Some of them spoke of seeing strange beings, and many referred to high-pitched, whining, machine-like sounds, very much like the laughter of the skull-face creature. It talked about the pineal gland, and suggested that it played a big role in psychedelic experiences.

I started seeing more references to the pineal gland in the articles I read. This gland is unique, sitting deep in the center of the brain, shaped like a pinecone and as small as a grain of rice. Rene Descartes called the pineal gland "the seat of the soul." Other philosophers along with scientists have been fascinated with this gland for centuries. I realize now it was the source for everything that happened to me, starting with the visions.

The little girl in purple said my pineal gland was a doorway for demons. The skull-face creature knew this. The more I researched, and the more visions that came, I came to accept that creature was a demon from another world. And it won't leave me alone. I'm so afraid it's going to take me, Dr. Steiner. It's just a matter of time. It already took my

The Dark Gland

voice. That was the most frightening part that I haven't told you about yet. But I have to, so you'll know how terrified I am.

I'd fallen asleep on the sofa after watching TV. I woke up suddenly, and the lights were off. I sat up and flipped the switch on the wall next to me, and nothing came on. I hit the remote but the TV screen wouldn't turn on either. Then a clap of thunder and a streak of lightning filled the room.

I felt relieved knowing it was just one of those New England storms that came out of nowhere and took out the power. I was thirsty, and carefully made my way over to the fridge. I opened the door and felt around for the juice and took a swig. When the fridge door fell closed, I noticed something reflected in the window.

When I walked over to the window, something moved behind me. I turned around, and nothing was there. When I turned back, a streak of lightning lit the sky, and its reflection was in the window. It was standing behind me, that horrible creature, its skull-face grinning at me. I screamed and it grabbed me, and suddenly I wasn't in my apartment anymore. I was flying through the window. I looked back and there was my body lying on the floor of my living room, but I wasn't inside of it anymore.

I was taken to the outer space I'd seen in my mind, traveling through the bright streaks and stars, zigzagging and crisscrossing, everything spinning, and then it stopped.

I was in a place that seemed like a giant dark cloud. All around me was a dense darkness that felt more like nothingness. I tried to scream but no sound came out. The ground beneath me was solid but soft. It enveloped my backside and formed around my hips. I was sinking. It felt like I was being swallowed by a giant beanbag chair. I thought this must be what it feels like to be inside a black hole.

There were murmurs all around me. Soft, muffled voices that I couldn't understand. Maybe they were speaking another language. I was so scared. Every time I tried to scream, shout, make any sort of noise, nothing would come out. Hands grabbed at me from all angles, though they weren't really hands because there were no fingers. They were more like gobs of flesh.

Then the tiniest shimmer of light appeared above me. It felt wonderful, and then a clear, high-pitched voice started to hum. The light grew, the gobs of flesh went away and the dark murmurs stopped. I was moving through the streaks and stars again, spinning in the opposite direction. I saw the giant little girl in purple and she spoke to me.

"If you come back to this place, they will take you forever."

Then I was on the floor of my living room, the power was on, the television showing an infomercial. I'd never felt such relief before, and started to laugh thinking it was just some crazy vivid dream. But when I tried to laugh, no sound came out. I tried to speak, shout, hum, whistle, but nothing happened.

My voice was gone. I felt sick and ran to the bathroom. I caught a glimpse of myself in the mirror, and there were two streaks of white hair starting at my temples.

Dr. Steiner, I'm so afraid this skull-face demon will take me back to that dark land. The pills help in keeping the demon away. They help me block out the demon in my dreams, but sometimes its face appears before they kick in, and I turn on my little book light. It's been helping, so far.

The Dark Gland

But it's better to have the lights on all the time. It only shows up in the dark, and when darkness is all around me, the demon is there, just waiting for its chance to take me.

I tried to explain to my boyfriend what happened to me. He thought I was showing him a sci-fi story, that I was trying my hand at creative writing. The look of pity on his face when he saw my hair was something I'll never forget. I never want anyone to look at me like that again.

My mother didn't believe me. She said I was lying about losing my voice to get out of work. I wanted her to read the same thing I showed my boyfriend, but she tore it up and threw it away. Then she called you guys at McLean. At least in this place, they don't look at me with pity.

Do you believe me? I'm telling you the truth of what happened, why I can't sleep without those wonderful pills the nurses bring, and why I need the lights on. I'm sure you'll say it's something I hallucinated, or that it's schizophrenia or something. Or I'm making it up to get out of the real world and stay in a hospital where I don't have to deal with anything. That's what my mother thinks. She doesn't think I'm actually crazy, but I bet a lot of people do.

Am I crazy, Dr. Steiner? I guess that's your job, the final diagnosis to the level of my craziness. Your job is to help me, right? Keeping the lights on is a good start, but it's not the solution. I need to find a way to keep this demon from getting to me, and I think I know how.

I need to keep that doorway closed for good. Keep that dark gland of mine from bringing demons into this world. My pineal gland is a portal, and I need to stop it from working. Can you just remove it from my brain? Is that even possible, a pineal lobotomy?

You're a doctor and you know about things that my mother and boyfriend don't. You've studied medicine and the mind and maybe you've had patients like me before. I hope you can help me. I don't want the demon to take me away for good.

*****

Rachel stopped writing and flipped through the pages in the journal. The burnt sienna crayon had worn down a few pages in and the words went from periwinkle to olive green.

After Rachel handed in her journal to Dr. Steiner, who smiled in that condescending way some doctors do, she went back to her room and sat on the bed. She hoped Dr. Steiner would not only keep the lights on in her room after he read it, but increase her dosage of pills as well.

Though she was exhausted from writing and wanted to lie down, she hadn't had her evening dose and wouldn't dare fall asleep without it.

The minutes ticked by and the nurse still hadn't arrived with her pills. Rachel yawned and stood up, paced around the room, and noticed the sun going down for the evening. She watched the sky turn from reddish-orange to light purple, and the nurse still hadn't shown up. Rachel sighed and went to the door to listen.

A rumble of thunder was followed by a streak of lightning near the maple tree. Rachel shuddered, and when the rain began to pound against the window she stepped back with a shiver. Another band of lightning flashed and suddenly all of the lights went out.

Rachel yelped and ran back to the window. It was dark everywhere. A power outage wasn't something she'd worried about in a big hospital with generators, and she rushed over to her nightstand and bumped her shin on the bedframe.

She felt around until she found the little drawer to the nightstand and yanked it open. She reached in and felt the flat plastic of her book light and turned it on.

It only offered a tiny beam of light, and Rachel wondered how long it would be before the backup generators came on. Then something flashed before her eyes. She jumped, and something smacked the book light out of her hand. The light went out.

Muffled voices and rustling noises surrounded her. She heard faint chanting in a language she didn't recognize, and snapping noises like tree branches breaking.

There was a flash of lightning, and then streaks of blue light and swirling beams of orange swam before her eyes. The skull-face of the creature appeared through the colors and smiled at her.

"Rachel..." it said her name in a raspy hiss. It grabbed her, repeatedly hissing her name.

Rachel tried to hit the hands that grasped her, but her fists went right through them as if they were wisps of smoke. Yet they held onto her tightly like slimy ropes, and wrapped around her arms and legs.

Then she was flying through the stars of outer space, spinning through colors that grew darker by the second. She found herself sitting in the dark place she'd been taken to before.

Darkness enveloped her. She sank deeper into it, her legs and arms covered in thick dark matter, making her part of the surface she sat upon. She opened her mouth to scream, hoping that her voice would come back briefly and allow her some form of release, but no sound came out. The dark matter filled in her mouth and covered her eyes. She was buried.

A second later the hospital generator came to life and the lights were back on, but Rachel's body remained frozen in her bed. When the nurse came in and saw Rachel's stiff body and no response when she tapped her shoulder, she rushed to bring Dr. Steiner into the room.

The doctor lifted Rachel's eyelids and flashed a penlight in front of them, then sighed and glanced down at her journal attached to his clipboard. The nurse picked up the broken book light from the floor.

"Catatonic Schizophrenia," Dr. Steiner whispered and shook his head.

He thought he heard a faint sound escape Rachel's mouth. He leaned forward with his ears perked, but all he could hear was the buzzing of the generator. He gave Rachel's pupils one more glance, sighed, and left the room.

He went back to his office and opened Rachel's journal. After he finished reading it he made a note to use excerpts from it in his next paper, cataloging the different hallucinations in schizophrenic patients.

Dr. Steiner found it interesting that two other patients had hallucinations similar to Rachel's. They even described seeing the face of the Grim Reaper, and feeling like there was a demon inside of them.

He stuck a sticky note on top of Rachel's journal. On the note, he wrote "Number Three Grim Reaper." He thought perhaps there was enough material to turn the paper into a book.

The Sublime Life

Deke turned down the volume when the song came blasting through the radio. He couldn't believe it was another Sublime song, the third one this station had played that morning. It had been over four years since the lead singer Bradley Nowell died, and so many stations constantly played Sublime. It was as if his death made the music more popular.

He could've sworn it was the same song, too, though all Sublime songs sounded alike to him. And often times he'd hear what he thought was a Sublime song, ended up being a 311 song. They all sounded alike to him, too.

Deke shook his head and turned the radio off. He sat down at the computer and stared at the blank screen in front of him, the cursor blinking in that teasing way. Off on, off on, now you see it, now you don't, just like the magic trick writing is. Maybe this is the day an epic poem is begun, or perhaps it's an entire day spent working on a story that goes nowhere. Writing is part talent, part learned skill, and mostly blood, sweat and tears. Deke's roommate Albert taught him that, back when Albert was Professor Gould and Deke was a first-year student in his writing class.

Deke sighed and rested his forehead against the monitor. He had an idea for a new story, and had lots of time in front of him to work on it, but nothing was coming out. He hated it when that happened. He sometimes wondered if he was really a writer, or just someone else's misplaced muse.

When he thought of Albert's encouragement and the small, obscure journals that had published his work, he knew it was just a case of writer's block. Albert wanted him to send his writing to a publishing house or a magazine with a larger circulation like *The New Yorker*, but Deke didn't want to.

When he agreed to move in with Albert, he thought it had been a good idea at the time. He'd always liked Albert, but after moving in with someone you start learning their idiosyncratic routines. And sometimes, you don't like them anymore, such as how Albert liked to stand up and eat crackers by the counter. Deke couldn't understand why Albert didn't sit down at the table while he ate. He also got crumbs all over the floor.

Deke sighed and looked up, and gazed through the window. The view of his neighbor's curtains wasn't exactly inspiring, but it was certainly better than seeing him dry off after a shower, which he had a tendency to do with the curtains open.

The sky was hazy, an opaque grayish color that resembled mother-of-pearl in that it changed color depending on how the sun shone through. Though the colors of smog weren't nearly as pleasant as the pearl used for jewelry and brooches.

Deke lived in Long Beach, and he didn't like it. He thought he should live somewhere on the east coast, like New York or Boston. He didn't have the right disposition for sunny Southern California. With his dark hair and pale skin that never tanned, he didn't have the right look for it either.

He didn't even live close enough to the ocean to have a nice view. There was something inspiring about having a room with a view of water. It was far more inspiring than a view of the building next door, which had been his typical view in everywhere he'd lived since college.

Deke turned back to the monitor and minimized the new document he'd opened. He went into another folder and opened up the piece he was working on the night before.

Flight

by Deacon Muller

It was another damn Sublime song playing through the speakers. Those songs bug me more than hearing a Lynyrd Skynyrd song, or a Nirvana song because of how that guy died right before their biggest album was released. At least those other guys enjoyed a bit of stardom before dying.

I always thought that was the ultimate "fuck you." Not only dying young, but dying when you're at the height of your career. So many people had that awful fate. James Dean. Jimi Hendrix. Tupac Shakur. Kurt Cobain. People don't like it when I compare him because he committed suicide, but if you ask me, the others just did it in different ways with the lifestyles they led. Tupac lived the Thug Life. James Dean liked to drive fast. Same with the ones who overdose. It's all the same thing, isn't it? That death wish gene. Some people have it, and some people don't. I don't have it, but I'm worried all the time about death, and dying. Some people say I'm obsessed, but I say I'm just preparing for the inevitable.

Jenna Moquin

This is the sort of shit I think about when I'm trying to fall asleep at night.

****

If I were the author of this story, I would tell him to just kill himself. Just do it, like your mother did.

Deke felt a shiver as he read the last couple of lines, the ones he'd jotted down underneath the asterisks. It was one of those afterthought lines he sometimes wrote, that was in between the narrator's point of view, and the character's point of view. He'd been experimenting with this metafiction writing style since he began reading Kurt Vonnegut last year.

There was something eerie about that last line in particular, because in that story, there wasn't a mother who committed suicide. He didn't recall writing it, but being a writer he certainly didn't recall every single line he'd ever written. He figured he wrote it while he'd been nodding off at the computer, which was a habit of his. He was probably thinking about his own mother as he was falling asleep.

Claudia May was an author, and achieved moderate success as a ghost writer for a famous young girl's mystery series for some time. She had always encouraged Deke's writing. She and Deke used to write poems together, and would take turns reciting them for Hank, Deke's father. As Deke grew older, and more serious about his craft, they did writing exercises together.

One was a speed-writing competition to see who could write the most words in under ten minutes using randomly selected themes. Deke's favorite was when Claudia closed her eyes while she thumbed through a thick novel like *Anna Karenina*, picked out ten random words, and they'd write a ten-line poem with one of those words in each line.

A few years into her career as a writer, Claudia was contacted by an agent who wanted her to write a mystery series for television, and the pilot was a hit. Two months after it premiered, she was diagnosed with pancreatic cancer.

He remembered the look on his mother's face when she came home from the hospital. It was a look he'd never seen before. His mother always had a confidence about her that most people didn't. She carried herself in a way that commanded respect, and everyone did respect her. But when she came home from the hospital that day, she had a look on her face that made her look like a completely different person. She looked defeated. Deke cried himself to sleep that night.

Two weeks later Claudia hanged herself in the garage. Her husband Hank was the one who found her. Deke had been twelve at the time.

With a strong exhale through his nostrils Deke pushed his chair backward and it scraped against the floor. He stood up and went over to the open window. He was three stories up.

He looked down to the street, and wondered if a fall from this height would take him out. Or, if he would simply become paralyzed, possibly no longer able to write. That would be a fate worse than death to Deke, and he was afraid enough of death as it was.

He avoided amusement park rides, traveled as little as possible, and covered himself in sunblock whenever he went outside, which wasn't often unless he was going to work or the grocery store.

He knew death was something inevitable, like inclement weather and menstruation, but he still didn't want to invite it any sooner by risking his life.

Though he longed for a place with a nice view of the ocean, he wasn't a huge fan of the outdoors. Aside from getting easily sunburnt, he didn't like being in a place where he couldn't lock himself away in a bedroom or bathroom if he needed to be alone. Albert thought he had a touch of agoraphobia.

He saw Albert walking toward the front steps. They shared Deke's Toyota but it needed a new radiator, so they were reduced to walking and public transportation for the time being, which could be rough in southern California. Deke stuck his hand out and waved at him, but he wasn't sure if Albert saw him since he didn't wave back.

Deke was about to turn back inside when he saw the guy who lived in the apartment below him and Albert. He lived with an older man, but they weren't a couple just like Deke and Albert weren't. Albert liked to joke that those two roommates were the dorky versions of the two of them.

Deke had never gotten a good look at the younger guy, but he did seem to be about his height and had the same dark hair and pale skin, at least from what he could see three stories up.

He turned away from the window and as soon as he did it slammed shut behind him. Deke's heart pounded as he inspected the glass. There was a hairline crack near the corner of the pane.

He opened and closed the window to see how loose it was. He closed it tightly and shrugged his shoulders. He opened the door to let in Albert, who still didn't have his own set of keys.

The Sublime Life

There had been times when Deke came home to find Albert sprawled in front of the door at the top of the stairs, sleeping and snoring, waiting for Deke to come home with the keys. He just kept forgetting to get his own set made.

Albert had picked up the mail from downstairs and tossed it on the table. Deke noticed the return address on one of the envelopes was the logo from Orange County University. He flinched. Their old school was a bit of a sore subject.

Albert had been fired from the University for sleeping with two female students who made complaints that he'd seduced them. Deke suspected what they were really upset about was that Albert hadn't given them good grades after they slept with him. Albert said he thought the girls had sex with him because they wanted to, and he gave them fair grades based on the work they handed in. It didn't go over well with the school administration, though, or the parents of the girls.

He'd stood by Albert's side, along with several of his students. The ex-boyfriend of one of the girls came forward and said that she had bragged about "banging teachers to get good grades," but still Albert had been dismissed, despite his tenure.

Deke stuffed the envelope underneath the rest of the mail. He didn't know if it was for him or Albert, but suspected it was probably just one of those alumni donation letters. They still kept sending them to Albert, too. Deke thought the school had a lot of gall for that.

He hadn't been able to get a job teaching anywhere. Deke tried to get him a job at the Waldenbooks where he worked, but his manager happened to be friends with the parents of one of the girls Albert slept with at OCU. It actually got Albert blacklisted from Waldenbooks in four different malls in the area.

Albert was currently working part-time at a small used book store a few blocks from their apartment. The book store specialized in vintage erotic literature, and videos. Deke browsed through the store at one point and saw dog-eared copies of books with half-naked women on the covers. He told Albert that online pornography was going to take over eventually, but Albert didn't believe him. He didn't think people would be willing to give up their privacy over what sort of porn they liked by leaving an electronic paper trail, so he was convinced that stores like his would prevail.

"Write anything good today?" Albert said as he broke open a beer from the six pack he'd brought in with the mail. Deke took a beer for himself.

"Not much."

After finishing the six pack with Albert and talking trash about OCU and women in general, Albert sauntered off to bed and Deke decided to stay up and try to use the buzz he'd gotten from the beer. He enjoyed writing after having a couple of beers or a glass of wine, and after reading it the next morning would be pleasantly surprised at how good it was. But a drink or two was all he'd allow himself. He was too afraid of getting used to the buzz and then needing it.

After a while, a glass or two wouldn't do anything and he'd have to drink more, or perhaps move on to some stronger substance. Many writers and musicians had overdosed, and Deke was so afraid of going down that same road that he'd never even tried smoking pot. Some people, including Albert, had suggested he use it to cure his insomnia, which was something he suffered from often.

Instead, whenever he had trouble sleeping he would stay up all night writing, and sometimes went without sleeping for a few days until he was so tired he passed out.

The next morning, Deke felt the crick in his neck before he felt the stickiness of the paper stuck to his cheek with drool. He sat up and tore the paper off his face. He'd fallen asleep while writing again.

He moved the mouse to bring the monitor back to life and looked at the screen. The last thing he recalled writing was the description of his character's apartment, which was a very similar description of his own apartment.

He scrolled up, and there were several pages he didn't remember writing. There was also some dialogue between his main character and his girlfriend about where they were meeting for dinner.

Deke blinked. He hadn't created a girlfriend for his protagonist.

"Where the hell did she come from?" Deke scrolled up a few more pages and read.

He had somehow added a character named Denise, and wrote over a dozen new pages. He didn't recall writing any of this. He read the rest of the scenes and the dialogue, they weren't half-bad.

After the last paragraph, there were some lines a few spaces down, in smaller font. Deke leaned in closely to read.

why don't you just fucking kill yourself? just do it already. you're going to die soon, you goddamn well know it, so why don't you do the job yourself? take that power back. take the gun, jump the bridge, do whatever you gotta do. just fucking do it already.

Deke pushed back in his chair. He was breathing in sharp gasps, his heart pounding.

"I didn't write that," he whispered. "Did I?"

He stood up and felt how much he needed to use the toilet. He rushed over to the bathroom and relieved himself as he tried to digest what had happened.

He'd heard of people sleepwalking, but not sleep-writing. It concerned him that he would be alert enough to coherently type scenes and dialogue with proper punctuation and grammar, but not alert enough to remember doing it. It concerned him even further that he would write something like that last paragraph.

He flushed and looked at himself in the mirror. The gray hairs at his temples looked new. He didn't recall these gray hairs in his head just like he didn't recall writing those scenes.

Then he remembered the beer. Deke's face lit up and he smiled. He felt better realizing the alcohol had simply made him black out. And gray hairs were just a natural part of the aging process.

He went into the kitchen and opened the refrigerator. Save for a jar of pickles and a moldy carton of Chinese food, it was empty. The beer was gone, and he was glad for that. He wouldn't drink again, at least not for a while. He didn't even get the deep sleep that usually came with drinking because he'd fallen asleep at the computer, and his neck was still sore.

He glanced at the mail on the table, sorted into two piles. He saw his name on the top envelope in the pile on the left and picked it up. It was from *Modern Fiction*, one of his favorite magazines. He assumed it was to renew his subscription and opened it.

Deke read the letter. The first line said, "We have read 'Origins of Man' and would like to include it in next month's edition." He had to read it twice to let it sink in.

He dropped the letter onto the table. "Origins of Man" was a novella he'd completed a few months ago. It was about a boy who finds his father hanging from the ceiling in the attic, and the boy runs away from home and embarks on a journey across the Pacific Northwest. He lives in the wilderness for several years.

The letter went on to say that due to its length, they wanted to publish the story in two parts. Deke's mind was reeling. He felt like he'd stepped into another dimension, someone else's life, not his.

Modern Fiction was considered the *Reader's Digest* of fiction. He didn't want his writing to be published in something that big. But somehow the editors had gotten hold of his story. He couldn't figure out how, unless he was sleep-submitting his work like he was sleep-writing the night before.

Then he glanced down at the name Albert Gould in the other pile of mail.

"Albert!" Deke shouted.

He stormed out of the kitchen and went into Albert's room. He wasn't there. There was a pile of dirty laundry on the floor. Deke kicked it. He stuffed the letter from *Modern Fiction* into his pocket and left the apartment.

He checked the bookstore where Albert worked, but he wasn't there. He went to the library, the diner on Del Coronado Road, but he wasn't at any of his usual haunts.

He decided to check the bookstore again, since it was on his walk home anyway. He went around to the parking lot in the back where Albert sometimes smoked cigarettes or joints.

Albert was standing by the dumpster puffing away on a thin, crudely rolled blunt. He saw Deke and waved at him.

Deke walked up and shoved Albert against the dumpster. The blunt went flying.

"Why did you do that?" Albert threw his hands up in the air.

Deke pulled Albert toward him only to shove him against the dumpster again.

"What's wrong with you, man?" Albert's slowed reaction time caught up and he shoved Deke away from him. Deke stumbled and was short of breath.

"You sent in 'Origins of Man,' didn't you?"

"Holy shit, did the *L.A. Review* buy it?"

"*L.A. Review*? It was *Modern Fiction*. Jesus Albert, how many other places did you send it to?"

"Uh…just those two!" Albert shrugged.

"I told you, I fucking told you I didn't want to submit my writing!"

"But you sent it to *Stonehenge* and *The Pot Boiler*!"

"They're not fucking *Modern Fiction*! Or *L.A. Review*, Jesus, Albert!!"

Deke threw a punch in Albert's direction and then walked a few steps away. He shoved his hands into his pockets. He turned and stared at Albert.

"Don't you realize that any sort of success means my death?"

Albert shook his head.

"You're crazy, man. I thought you gave up on that coincidental crap in college."

"It's not a coincidence. It's a curse."

Deke walked away. Albert called after him, but he kept walking and quickened his step. He went to their apartment, and just as he reached the building the two roommates who lived downstairs, who Albert said were dorky versions of him and Deke, walked out.

They seemed to be in deep conversation, and Deke looked at the ground as he passed them. One of them said "Hello," and Deke nodded, keeping his head down. A few minutes after he got home, Albert came bursting through the door.

"What the hell has gotten into you?"

"Leave me alone." Deke went into his room. Albert followed him. Deke plopped onto his bed and covered his face with his pillow.

"You want me to hold that pillow down," Albert said. "And end it all for you, huh?"

Deke was silent. Albert leaned up against the wall and rolled his eyes.

"You can't live your life like this, man. It's not good. You're incredibly talented, Deacon Muller, and you should be proud of that, not afraid of it."

"You don't understand." Deke sat up and tossed the pillow to the floor.

"Is it more of that family curse crap? Because that's all just coincidences. That's all life is, man, a series of coincidences."

"So it's just a coincidence that my mother got cancer right after she got her big break? Or that my grandfather got run over by a bus three days into his retirement?"

"Deke, those aren't even coincidences—that's just bad luck!"

"So Nowell and Larson both dying on the twenty-fifth day of the month, four months apart, is nothing but bad luck as well?"

"Yes," Albert said with a sigh. This was a familiar conversation, one they'd had several times in the past. Usually after a few beers, and some weed on his part.

"It's not just the dates that make them similar." Deke sat up straighter and Albert groaned. "They both died right before they got big. Jonathan Larson died right before *Rent* premiered, and Bradley Nowell died right before Sublime released their biggest album. That's like the ultimate 'fuck you!' from God."

"Deke, I've said it a million times before. Death sells. *Rent* drew a huge audience because people knew the composer had died suddenly, it made them want to see it. Sublime got so popular because people were shocked about the drug overdose. Look at how Nirvana's sales increased after Kurt Cobain died! Same thing with Tupac."

"You're living in fear, man…you gotta let it go!"

Deke shook his head. "You still had no right to send in my work without my permission."

"You're right. I'm sorry. But you have to let go of this. It's only coincidences…bad luck! Random shit that just happens."

Deke looked away so Albert couldn't see him roll his eyes.

"And congrats on getting into *Modern Fiction*, man. That's something to be proud of."

Albert patted him on the shoulder and Deke nodded, still with his head turned toward the wall. Albert left and closed the door behind him. Deke turned to lay on his back and stared at the ceiling instead of the wall.

There were lots of coincidences that Deke didn't think were the sorts of things that just happened. It wasn't just the deaths in his family, or the coincidental ones surrounding famous people. He believed there was an order to it, connections in dualities. The Hoover Dam connection was one that Deke had always found eerie.

The Sublime Life

J.G. Tierney was a surveyor for the Hoover Dam and died on December 20, 1922 while looking for an ideal spot to build the dam. He fell off a barge and drowned, and was considered the first of many deaths associated with the Hoover Dam Project. His son Patrick Tierney died on December 20, 1935, by falling off the dam's intake tower. He is considered to be the last death associated with the project. They died on the same day of the month, just like Bradley Nowell and Jonathan Larson.

Then there was the King Umberto story, which many Italians claim to be true. When Deke first heard it he felt chills all over. King Umberto I of Italy met a man who looked exactly like him, a restauranteur also named Umberto. He not only looked just like him but they had the same birthday, and their wives had the same name. The next day, Umberto the restauranteur was accidentally killed while cleaning his gun. Soon after King Umberto heard the news of his death, he was assassinated. It made Deke think about the old superstition that meeting your doppelgänger was an omen for death, for both of you, and he feared one day meeting his. That was why he didn't like bumping into his downstairs neighbor. He didn't even like looking into mirrors.

This fear was with him every day when he woke up. It made him stay indoors and never travel, never take chances. This fear seemed to be slowly taking over his life. Sometimes, Deke wondered if the only way to deal with the fear, was to take the power back by taking his own life.

He'd always known that he wasn't going to live to be an old man. He couldn't explain it, but it was something he'd felt for years. He knew he would die young, just like his mother had.

Many writers had died young, including two of his greatest influences, Edgar Allen Poe and Ernest Hemmingway. Deke also enjoyed the poetry of Sylvia Plath, who attempted suicide a couple of times before being successful at it. He wondered if she had the same fears he did, and wanted to take that power back too.

He'd come to accept that's what his mother had done. She felt like she'd lost control when the cancer was discovered, and she took control back by taking her own life. She was doing something inevitable, anyway. She just did it on her own time.

Deke stood up. Whenever thoughts like that came into his head he wanted to write them down, or write about something, anything to get them to stop. He went to the computer and turned it on. While he waited for it to boot up he grabbed a notepad and pen to get things started. After he scribbled for a few minutes he looked down at what he'd written.

I don't write because I want to get famous. It would be nice, but it's not why I do it. I do it, like the majority of other writers out there, because I have to. There's something inside of me that wants to get out, thoughts and ideas forming into characters and stories that swarm around my head so much that I sometimes can't sleep at night.

Sirens blared from the street below, and seconds afterward more sirens and fire engines. Deke wanted to close the windows but it was too hot in the apartment, so he turned on the radio.

And a Sublime song was playing.

Deke shuddered and shook his head. He turned the knob. Loud static came through until he found a different station playing the Lenny Kravitz cover of "American Woman."

He sighed and stared at the monitor before typing. He was having trouble getting into a zone, there were too many thoughts swirling around his head. The noises from the street were distracting, but he focused on the screen and forced himself to write. As he typed, the Lenny Kravitz song ended. Then Deke heard the opening chords to the exact same Sublime song the last station had been playing.

Deke shook his head and looked at the radio. He could've sworn the volume was louder, the same way it was louder when commercials came on. He turned off the radio and sat down. He typed for a few minutes and then cupped his chin in his hands to read what he'd written.

I know I'm going to die the same way that guy from Sublime did. I'll become famous after I die, like so many others. It's one of my biggest fears aside from being buried alive. But if I had to pick, I'd choose dying like that over being buried alive.

He heard the shower running in the bathroom. He'd forgotten Albert was home. He was pretty loud between talking at the television and the noisy way he fiddled with the pages while he read a book, but when Deke couldn't hear Albert, it usually meant that he was reading a different kind of book, the kind where he wasn't fiddling with the pages because he was fiddling with himself.

Deke chuckled. It had been a while since Albert had a woman. It was one of the things they had in common. Deke had always had problems with women. Not only problems with getting them, but overall problems with them, like a lot of men he'd met. He'd had sex a handful of times, but found pleasing himself to be the most satisfying of all.

He'd been mistaken as being gay a couple of times in his life. He wasn't sure if it was something about the way he carried himself, or his fastidiousness. Perhaps it was the fact that he'd never had a steady girlfriend. He didn't really care, because he didn't think that people should be so concerned about what sort of pleasure got a fellow human being through the night, as long as they weren't hurting anyone else.

He got up and went to the kitchen, taking a look at the acceptance letter from *Modern Fiction*. His fears and worries aside, he had to admit it felt good to be accepted, and paid for his work, which he hadn't been before. Deke couldn't help but smile at that.

The shower stopped running, and a few minutes later Albert came out of the bathroom wearing a t-shirt and a towel wrapped around his bottom half. Deke was at the table opening the rest of his mail.

"Want to get Chinese tonight?" Albert asked.

"Sounds good." Deke waved the letter from *Modern Fiction* in the air. "I didn't read this carefully enough. Since they normally pay fifty bucks a story, and 'Origins of Man' is going to be published as a two-parter, they're paying me a hundred fucking dollars for it."

Deke wagged his eyebrows up and down and grinned at Albert, who came over and gave him a high-five.

"Food's on me!" Deke laughed. "And this'll help get the Toyota fixed."

Albert picked up a six-pack of beer along with the food, but Deke declined in having any. He didn't want a repeat of the night before.

While they ate, Albert told him how much he liked "Origins of Man."

"Thanks," Deke said through a mouthful of noodles.

"What's this new one you're working on about?"

"It's about a guy who's afraid of dying right when he becomes famous, and is haunted by hearing Sublime songs all the time. At the end of the story, he kills himself, right before he gets big."

"Man, I like that. I like how the moral of the story is sometimes you're your own worst enemy."

"Thanks."

"Plus, you're writing about your own fears. That can be like a cathartic session with a shrink, man."

"I guess that's a good point. I do write about my own fears, I think lots of writers do. It's a way of dealing with the fear."

"I've heard that too."

"But it doesn't always work out that way. Sometimes it helps with the fears, but it doesn't make them go away."

Albert took a sip of beer and belched. They finished eating and Albert took the rest of the six-pack into his room, after checking with Deke to make sure he was really all set with having anymore beer.

Deke sat at the computer and spent the next couple of hours typing until he fell asleep on top of the keyboard. He didn't wake up until the next morning when Albert shook him to get ready for work. He went to Waldenbooks that day tired and sore from sleeping in a strange position.

He thought about *Modern Fiction*, and he was getting excited over the prospect of a book contract, or an agent interested in representing him. He knew it was only one novella, but it was very promising. His fears and worries aside, the thought of being a professional writer was the most sublime life he could imagine, as long as he didn't have the same fate as the guy from Sublime.

Getting paid a hundred dollars for his work was definitely something to write home about, and he thought about his father. He hadn't visited his father much since he'd left for college. After Claudia died, Hank fell into a depression that lasted for the rest of the time Deke lived with him. He barely spoke to Deke, and simply went through the motions each day. Deke had won writing competitions in high school, and Hank hadn't attended any of the ceremonies.

After Deke went off to college, Hank donated most of the money Claudia left to cancer research, bought a houseboat and moved to the San Francisco Bay area. Deke spent holidays and summers on campus.

Deke thought about calling his father to tell him about his story, but he didn't want to bring up any subject that would remind him of Claudia. He decided to keep this news to himself, at least for the time being.

After work, Deke went down to the beach and sat on the stone wall near the bike path. He watched a group of skaters roll down the pier, one of them held a boom box. One of the things he hated about California was that nearly every decent spot for solitude was outdoors, though he did enjoy looking at the ocean. There was something soothing about it. He really would love one day to have a view of the ocean, or some other body of water. He could admire it from the safety of his bedroom window.

The skaters were leaving the pier, and heading his way down the bike path. The one holding the boom box fiddled with the knobs. Deke couldn't make out the song that was playing but it certainly sounded like a Sublime song. Or maybe it was a 311 song. He shook his head and stood up to walk home, and saw his doppelgänger standing before him.

The Sublime Life

He looked exactly like Deke. Dark shaggy hair, lanky frame, skinny with a sallow complexion and an unshaven beard. He even wore a torn black t-shirt like Deke. He took a step backward, his mouth moving up and down. Deke couldn't make out what he was saying.

"Mwaah mwahhh!"

The man pointed at Deke. Then he looked down at the man's worn shoes and shabby pants, and the cup in his other hand that he began to shake. The sound of coins jingling was shrill and made Deke shiver. He reached into his pocket and took out a wrinkled dollar bill and put it into the homeless man's cup.

He nodded at Deke and went over to a shopping cart filled with junk and pushed it away. He kept making that same "mwaahh" noise as he trotted away with the shopping cart.

Deke's heartbeat was racing so fast he could feel the vibrations in his chest. He had forgotten to breathe while he was staring at the man who looked just like him, and he gasped for air.

He leaned back against the wall to catch his breath before walking home, making sure to stay in crosswalks and look both ways. He didn't feel safe until he was back in his bedroom. He went to bed before the sun went down.

The next morning he woke up at noon. He jumped out of bed and then remembered he had the evening shift, and didn't have to be at work for a few hours. He relaxed in front of the television and ate leftover noodles out of the carton.

Deke was getting ready for work when Albert came home. He said he wanted to talk to him.

"Okay, now don't freak out, but…"

Deke looked at Albert with a sigh. Whenever he began a sentence like that, it wasn't good news. It usually meant he was going to be late with the rent, or needed to borrow some money. He took a bottle of iced tea from the fridge while he waited for Albert to continue.

"I sent in your latest manuscript to Simon & Schuster."

"What? What manuscript?"

"I saw it on your desk. All four hundred pages were next to the computer, title page and everything. I figured you were planning on sending it in, so I helped you out man. Even bound it for you!"

Albert held up his hand offering a high-five. Deke stared at him and blinked. Albert let his arm drop.

"Sorry, I thought I was doing you a favor."

"Albert…" Deke cleared his throat. "I didn't even turn on the computer last night. I went to bed early, and woke up at noon."

"Really, man?"

"And I haven't written anything that big for a while. I definitely don't remember printing off four hundred pages. The printer didn't jam, or anything?"

"I have no idea, I just saw it there. Maybe it was something you wrote a while back?"

"What was the title?"

"*Flight.*"

Deke dropped the bottle of iced tea to the floor. It rolled toward the stove.

"What the hell? 'Flight' is a short story I started a few days ago. You sure it was a full-length novel?"

"Yeah man, it was pretty fucking great too. I read it in one sitting, couldn't put it down. The inner dialogue was almost Salinger-like."

"You serious?"

"And you have these little metafiction Vonnegut elements thrown in. One of the best things you've ever written, maybe even the best."

Deke shook his head. He left the kitchen and went over to the computer. Albert followed him.

He opened "Flight." The last time he recalled making a note of the word count it was somewhere around seven thousand. When he opened it up now, *Flight* was 101,513 words.

Deke felt every pore in his body secrete sweat. His heartbeat slowed at first, then quickened and thudded in his ears.

"Albert," Deke croaked out. His mouth was dry. "I have no recollection of writing this."

"Come on, man, you're exaggerating."

"No. I'm not."

Deke shook his head and grabbed a tissue from the box on the shelf above him. He wiped his forehead, and a tiny piece of tissue paper remained stuck to his temple.

"Give me a little while to read this. Do you mind?"

"No, not at all." Albert backed up and left the room.

He waited until Albert left the apartment, then took a deep breath and read the first few pages, the ones he remembered writing days ago. He got to the part when the girlfriend he didn't recall creating showed up, and he turned off the monitor.

Albert said it was the best thing he'd ever written. J.D. Salinger quality. With elements of Kurt Vonnegut. He didn't think he had it in him to write something like that, but he had no recollection of writing it anyway.

Deke rushed into his bedroom and went to the bookshelf. He pulled out two three-ring binders and set them down on the dresser, then pulled out three more binders.

He opened the first binder to the title page. *Green River* was the first novel he'd ever written, somewhat of an expounded version of "Origins of Man."

He opened up another binder. The title *In Coconut Bay* made him cringe. He'd never been a big fan of that one, especially the title. The rest of the binders contained the other novels he'd written over the years. He certainly remembered writing these ones.

Deke, like some other writers, didn't think his writing was as good as people told him it was. He sometimes suspected people were just being nice. But after *Modern Fiction* had accepted his work, he'd grown a bit more confident.

Though how he'd written an entire novel that he had no memory of writing, that was so good his former English professor told him it was on level with classic authors, was cause for concern.

He looked at the yellow sticky note thumb-tacked to his wall. The thumbtack was there because the sticky note had been re-attached to so many different places over the years (walls, pieces of paper, calendars), that it was no longer sticky. It was really just a little yellow square piece of paper.

Miriam Suffolk, Ph.D., Psy.D

And had a phone number scribbled beneath it. Dr. Suffolk was a psychiatrist Deke had visited a few times. He recalled copying her name from the business card, and then wondering why he'd bothered to put in the suffixes. Perhaps it was how he liked that her surname sounded like the word suffix.

The Sublime Life

The first time he was in her office he made a crack, something along the lines of "Dr. Miriam Suffolk and her suffixes." She had given him a tight-lipped smile. He wondered how many times she'd heard that one. She was very nice, but he wasn't making much progress as he didn't feel comfortable talking about his mother's death. He never had.

He wondered if it was time to pay Dr. Suffolk another visit. He sighed as he stared at the phone number. He looked at the clock, it was past five. Her office would be closed anyway, and he was running late for work.

After he got dressed and placed his nametag in his pocket, he grabbed his keys and glanced at the computer with a sigh. He would have to wait to read the rest of *Flight*, if at all. Part of him was afraid to finish it. If it was as good as Albert said it was, and he didn't recall writing any of it, how could he say he'd written it? Even worse, how could he write something like it again?

Every writer fears losing the muse. Some people say certain authors have lost it over time and still keep producing subpar tomes and publishing them. Deke believed in quality over quantity. It was one of the reasons he admired writers like J.D. Salinger and Harper Lee.

He shook his head, and as he was turning around to leave the room the monitor came back on. The *Flight* manuscript stared at him from the screen. Deke stared at the monitor. He remembered turning it off—he didn't think it had been in screensaver mode. Even if it had, he hadn't touched the mouse.

He shook his head and told himself he must not have turned it off. It must have gone into screensaver mode as he was getting ready for work, and something jostled the desk enough to move the mouse. Maybe a big truck was driving by and shook the ground, made a vibration in the desk. Then he recalled the window shutting by itself the other day, and he shuddered.

As he walked over to the computer, he stared at *Flight* on the screen. The part in the manuscript that was staring back at him wasn't where he'd left off earlier. When he got closer he looked at the page number, it was on two hundred. He knew he hadn't scrolled down that far.

In the middle of page two hundred, a set of lines caught his eye, near a line of asterisks. His heartbeat quickened as he read.

That's what we do. We write about our fears as a way to deal with them. But it doesn't always work out that way, does it? Sometimes, the fears get worse.

****

Sometimes, the fears take over. Just like it will with the author of this story.

With shaking fingers he shut down the computer. He backed away from it, then shook his head and left the apartment. He went to work, happy to have something mechanical to focus on for the time being.

Deke went through the motions over the next few days. He wouldn't go near the computer. He wouldn't even pick up one of his notebooks and write. He went to work, took the Toyota to the shop, watched television, avoided Albert and ate dinner in his room. One night Albert

The Sublime Life

knocked on his door. Deke went to the door and opened it a crack.

"What's up?"

"Are you ever gonna come out of your room, man?"

"I come out all the time. Do you think I piss in here?"

Deke opened the door and walked past Albert into the kitchen. He opened the fridge and then slammed it shut.

"Do you ever buy food, Albert?"

"What's with you, Deke? Are you still upset I sent in that manuscript?"

"It's not just that you sent it in. I don't even remember writing it. That's what's freaking me out."

He thought of telling Albert about the monitor coming back on by itself, but he paused.

"I think you're freaking out over nothing, man. Lots of writers do this! I've heard stories about writers getting into some kind of zone where they don't even remember how much time has passed, next thing they know they look up and wrote dozens of pages. I mean, it happens!"

"You don't get it, Albert. I don't remember writing any of that. What if they want to sign me, and I can't do it again? It's not like I have any control over this!"

Albert sighed and clapped him on the back.

"You've got it in you, man. I know you do. You're just losing confidence in yourself, that's all, happens to every writer. And you've got that fear you've always had. You're so freaked out about dying that you never enjoy life. You've never once gone outside without sunblock on. You almost never go out, period! You never party, you never take chances…you've never even tried pot you're so worried about getting addicted to some other drug."

"So?"

"So, lighten up! Life is sublime, man, it's a beautiful thing. You need to appreciate each moment you get, the good stuff and the bad, because you never know when your number is up. Look at how Jonathan Larson died, too. Days before *Rent* was first seen off-Broadway, he went to two different hospitals complaining of chest pains. They sent him home saying it was stress and the flu, or something. The day before its first preview, he was found dead. Some undiagnosed heart condition. That poor dude went to two different hospitals, they both sent him home, and he died."

"I know, that was one of the worst things I'd ever heard. But what's that prove?"

"When your number is up, it's up, doesn't matter what you do. Hell, I don't even care that I lost my tenure and now work in a damn porno store. I still get up and enjoy each day like it was my last, because it just might be. But you can't live your life being constantly worried about it, man."

Deke shrugged and went back to his room. Albert shook his head and went to his own room. Later on that night Deke got up, and spent the rest of the night typing away at the computer.

A few days later Deke had the day off from work and Albert went to the bookstore, and he had the place to himself. He decided to read the manuscript he didn't remember writing, see if anything jogged his memory.

He had a flash of inspiration the moment he turned on the computer, and once it booted up instead of opening *Flight* he began typing something new. It was the sort of thing he would've written back when he and his mother had their speed-writing contests. He didn't really have a theme, but he'd gone with a flow of what it felt like to have writer's block.

The Sublime Life

The blank page is the bane of a writer's life, that stares us in the face and laughs at us, taunts us saying "you're not a writer, you suck!" We can't stop looking at it, we give in to it, we give into our paranoia and lose all confidence in ourselves, we fall into the despair that they call writer's block, only it should be called writer's blank, it's the bright white blank screen that stares up at us, and we stare at it for so long we start seeing flashes and floaters in our vision, little clear circles and tiny dots that swirl on the page, hypnotizing us, we sit and stare and can't write a word.

He was startled when he heard music that was so loud it sounded like it was in the room with him.

It was the same Sublime song.

He got up to see where it was coming from, and wondered if it was his neighbors, or maybe blasting through the speakers of a car outside.

He opened the window a few more inches and kept his ear perked. He didn't hear anything coming from the street below. It wasn't the neighbors, he could see the dark windows. His neighbors weren't home.

Deke turned his head. The song was coming out of his radio. He didn't remember turning it on. He walked over to it.

It wasn't on. He made sure by switching the knob on then off again, and then he turned the volume knob down all the way. The song never paused.

Deke's heart was pounding. He tore the radio from the shelf and threw it across the room.

The song didn't stop.

He ran over to the radio and kicked it. He could still hear the baseline of the song. He kicked it again with a scream, and then kicked it against the wall making a long black mark. Finally, the music stopped.

He looked at the computer. The *Flight* manuscript was up on the screen, not the piece he'd just been writing. Deke trembled as he backed up, and bumped into the wall behind him. He screamed and ran out of the apartment.

On his way down the stairs, he bumped into his downstairs neighbor. The one who Albert said looked just like him.

"Oh hey, sorry!" He laughed and stood in front of Deke.

Deke stared at him. It was like he was looking into a mirror. He was even more of a doppelgänger than the homeless man.

"I'm Ted. You're Deke, right?"

Ted held out his hand. Deke shook it. His palm was clammy, but Ted's was firm and dry. Deke felt sweat pouring down his neck.

"Wow, we could be twins!" Ted said. "That's crazy!"

"Yeah..." Deke swallowed a lump in his throat. "Crazy..."

"You lived in this building long?"

"No," Deke croaked. He wiped the back of his neck.

"Hot one today, huh?"

Deke nodded.

"You guys got air conditioning in there?"

Deke shook his head.

"We don't either...blows, huh?"

Deke shrugged.

"Anyway, we should all hang out sometime, maybe grab a beer or something."

Deke nodded. He waited for Ted to move aside on the stairs so he could continue his descent. He cleared his throat and Ted walked off to his own apartment, and Deke trotted outside.

The Sublime Life

He wasn't paying attention when he got to the street, and ran into the crosswalk without checking the traffic light.

"Look out!"

A woman shouted and the car coming toward Deke swerved to the left. It missed him by a few inches. Deke fell and scraped his knees on the pavement. He ran back inside and locked the door behind him.

He saw the busted radio on the floor, and looked at the computer. *Flight* was still up on the screen. He shook his head and felt tears in his eyes. For once in his life, coming home and locking the door behind him wasn't making him feel any better.

He went to his room and closed the door. He shimmied his bookshelf in front of it and sat on the bed. The tears fell but he remained silent as he cried. His eyes shined as he picked up the photograph of his mother that had fallen when he moved the bookshelf.

It was a blue suede frame she got at a craft fair. It used to hold a picture of Deke as an infant, but after she died he replaced it with a photograph of Claudia, taken when she was young long before she married Hank and had him. Deke loved that picture of her. She had this innocent, expectant smile on her face. She was sixteen, beautiful, and had her whole life in front of her. He held the photo and traced her face with his finger.

"I miss you so much."

He held the photo against his chest. He dozed off, and woke up when night had fallen. He put the photo of his mother on the nightstand, then moved the bookshelf back to where it was, unblocking the door.

He tore Dr. Suffolk's number from the wall and went to the phone in the kitchen. He dialed her number, and was met with a *beep beep beep* and a recorded voice that said "The number you have dialed is not in service."

He tried it again paying closer attention to the keypad. He got the same message. She must have switched offices. He crumpled the little yellow piece of paper into a tiny ball and threw it away with a sigh.

With everything that had happened, he didn't even feel safe in his own home. He didn't feel comfortable around his father, and felt he had nowhere else to go.

Ever since his mother died, he knew the same fate lay ahead of him. Deke wondered, in the same way he imagined his mother had, that taking your life into your own hands was a way to do something about it. A way to take control back, by taking the power away from fate.

Or perhaps the fate had always been that he would take his own life the same way his mother had, because it was in his genes. He had read that suicidal behavior was hereditary, just like cancer.

Deke left the apartment, took the Toyota and drove around for a while. He ran over a pothole and the passenger side tire blew. He pulled over and slammed his palms against the steering wheel.

"This stupid car is as cursed as I am," Deke said.

He got out and began walking. He wasn't far from the beach, and went over to the stone wall near the bike path. He reached down and picked up some rocks from the ground, and played with them by turning them over and over in his hands. He sat there for a while listening to the waves.

Deke stood up, and walked over to the pier. He filled up his pockets with the rocks. He stared down at the water with a smirk. He finally had a good view, something

The Sublime Life

inspiring. Looking at the ocean was so calming, it reminded him of the cyclical nature of life. And death.

He took a deep breath, started to make his way over the edge of the pier, and then hesitated. He closed his eyes and saw his mother's face. She was smiling at him, her face fading in and out.

He thought of his father in his houseboat, sitting in a dock in the San Francisco Bay. A living version of that Otis Redding song. He thought about Albert, and how he'd lost his career. If there were anyone in his life he should strive to be successful for, if for nothing else so that they could enjoy his success, it was those two. He wanted it for his mother, too. He knew she would've been proud of him.

He also wondered, as he had in the past, what if she had tried to fight cancer, and survived? Maybe she'd still be alive.

Deke looked down at the water, then closed his eyes again. He saw his mother, but her smile was fading. Her face began to fade away completely, until he opened his eyes and saw nothing but the water below.

He took a deep breath and stepped away from the pier's edge. He pulled out the rocks from his pockets and tossed them into the water. He turned and walked away.

He breathed the ocean air into his lungs with a smile. He looked up and saw what he thought was a twinkling star, but when it moved he realized it was just a plane traveling overhead. He shrugged and made a wish anyway.

He wished that no matter what happened to him, that people would enjoy reading his work and get some form of pleasure or entertainment, if not some enlightenment. That was all he really cared about, anyway.

As he walked home he remembered the Toyota. He'd need Albert's help with the flat tire. When he got closer to his street, he saw blue and red lights flashing. He rounded the corner, and there was a police car and an ambulance parked outside his building.

Deke went inside and walked up the stairs. He noticed his downstairs neighbor's door was wide open, and he heard voices inside. He trotted upstairs to his apartment, and the door was ajar. He inched it open and saw Albert standing in the kitchen smoking a joint.

"You're finally home! It's been so crazy, come in and shut the door!"

"What happened?"

"You know the guy who lives downstairs, the one who looks just like you? He's fucking dead!"

"What?" Deke's heartbeat quickened and he started to sweat.

"He was right outside the building and this car went up on the curb and hit him. I heard that the guy driving the car had a heart attack or something, and that's why he lost control. One of those freak accidents."

"Are you kidding me, Albert?"

"I wouldn't joke about something like this, man!"

"I can't believe it," Deke whispered and sat at the table. "I just met him for the first time tonight."

"I know, it's crazy!"

Deke began to shiver. His doppelgänger, whom he'd just met, was dead.

"But I do have some good news, man."

Albert walked over to the answering machine and played the message. It was a literary agent who was interested in *Flight*.

"Alright Deke!" He clapped his hands and whistled.

"Oh my God," Deke said. He was trembling all over.

"I know, man, it's fucking incredible!"

He pulled out two beers from the fridge and put them on the table. He went into Deke's room and looked at the half dozen novels Deke had written over the years.

"And I'm sure they'll wanna see anything else you've written."

Deke was still trembling at the table, his body covered in cold sweat.

"You know I've always liked this one called *In Coconut Bay*, even though you said you hated it."

Deke wasn't listening to Albert. He was listening to the music that was blasting through the speakers of a car driving by outside, the same Sublime song he had a feeling would be haunting him for a long time.

Deke hung his head and let the fear wash over him. It was almost comforting, like a worn-in t-shirt. He closed his eyes and saw his mother's face. She was smiling at him, and looked as happy as she did in the photograph of her at age sixteen.

Albert came back into the kitchen and opened up one of the beers.

"We'll celebrate tonight, and you're having a beer, I don't care what you say!"

Deke picked up the other beer and opened it. He took a sip, then tilted his head back and chugged half of it.

"What happened to the radio, by the way?" Albert asked.

"I'll tell you later. You know what? I think I'll smoke with you tonight."

"You serious?" Albert laughed.

"Yeah. Might as well live it up. Eat, drink, and be merry, for tomorrow we die, right?"

Albert laughed and began rolling a joint.

"You're gonna be huge, Deacon Muller, I can just feel it!"

Deke managed a small smile for Albert, but inside, he was terrified.

They clinked beers, and when Albert was done rolling the joint Deke took a puff from it. He took in some air as Albert instructed and coughed on the exhale, and heard another car driving by playing a Sublime song. Or maybe it was a 311 song.

Deke shook his head and laughed. He took some comfort in the thought that even if he did die soon, he would not only be with his mother again, he would never have to hear another Sublime song again.

JENNA MOQUIN is the author of *Deluded Blood*, and her writing has appeared in diverse magazines and journals. She is a member of the New England Horror Writers and The Boston Horror Society. Currently living in the Boston area, she is working on her latest story.

Made in the USA
Middletown, DE
04 December 2021

54195099R00136